ISLA AND
LUKE:
MAKE OR
BREAK?

By the same author

When Isla Meets Luke Meets Isla

ISLA AND LUKE: MAKE OR BREAK?

RHIAN TRACEY

BLOOMSBURY

First published in Great Britain in 2004 by Bloomsbury Publishing Plc
38 Soho Square, London, W1D 3HB

A CIP catalogue record of this book is available from the British Library

ISBN 0 7475 6649 6

All papers used by Bloomsbury Publishing are natural, recyclable products made
from wood grown in well-managed forests. The manufacturing processes
conform to the environmental regulations of the country of origin.

Printed in Great Britain by Clays Ltd, St Ives plc

1 3 5 7 9 10 8 6 4 2

For Cerys

ISLA

In your first year in sixth-form college you've to take four subjects an' they call these AS levels. I'm taking biology obviously, because of ma nursing, an' chemistry an' psychology, an' then for ma own interests an' something extra to do to make up ma numbers, English literature, which I liked at school, reading an' poetry an' all that there. I loved *Macbeth* – that was an excellent play, an' nothing to do with it being the 'Scottish play' as Luke claimed.

In ma second year I have to cut it down to the three serious contenders, an' they're called A2s. They used to be called A levels but they've dropped the 'levels' part, I've no idea why. Ma classes will be much smaller than at school, though I think this'll be a wee bit better as I might actually get ma teacher's attention every now an' the while. O'course no' having Andrew James in practically all ma lessons with him being a complete arse will help. He's no' coming to college. He's getting a job with his brother an' uncle, they've a painting an' decorating business.

When we had our careers interviews at school last year Andrew told the woman to sod off an' that he had it all sorted an' didna need any 'bird' patronising him with advice an' GNVQ options. Andrew reckons that he's really good at it, the painting an' decorating lark, an' has been doing it since he was able to walk an' talk, which knowing him was not so long ago. I canny imagine him having a job an' being told what to do by anyone, especially by his older brother Anthony, who didn't even last until GCSEs at our school. He was excluded before it got to the exams stage. He came into school drunk, allegedly, an' then chucked a beaker of acid from the lab on another lad's shirt, 'cos he supported Spurs instead of Arsenal. Mr Thomas, the science teacher, who supports no one other than his personal gods Einstein and Michael Faraday, went mental an' lifted Anthony by his shirt collar an' chucked him right out of the lab, down to Mr Bourgoine's, the Deputy Head.

Mr Bourgoine. A worse fate could never meet a pupil, in ma opinion. Entering into his dark, pungent office is a sure guarantee of sudden death, or in Anthony's case nausea, all over the rug, an' then exclusion, obviously. Apparently Anthony smashed one of Mr Bourgoine's crystal paperweights on his way out, having already spattered his carpet with Special Brew lager. Well, according to legend, anyway, probably circulated by Anthony himself.

So Andrew's off to join Anthony, who now insists, in a rather firm manner, that you call him Tony. I try not to speak to him at all, which should be easy to keep up as I wouldna employ Andrew to paint ma house, that's if I actually had one.

Maybe he's got the right idea though. I mean what'll I do if I don't pass ma biology? No' much of a nurse I'll make if I canny even get ma biology A level, A things, whatever they're after calling them now. Am I supposed to make a big successful career out of ma English literature? Which is no' a sensible subject to 'fall back on', as ma Dad keeps reminding me as I rapidly exit whichever room we happen to be in, as soon as he starts on his favourite subject, ma future. He seems to miss the point that it's actually *ma* future – at least it would be if he would stop havin' peace talks an' negotiations about it round the dinner table. Still, college'll be better than getting a job, and what could I do anyway? Work in ma dad's shop? No fear, I'd end up talking about the latest articles in *Woman's Own* an' the shocking price of a pint of milk these days. I'd rather do more exams if it means I get to keep ma sanity. An' see Luke.

I'm so relieved Luke's going to college as well, even though he's no' in any of ma classes or ma tutor group. That was a shock there, to learn that we would have to have tutor groups again, as if we were kids still. I thought all that 'tutor group is an extension of your family' shite was reserved for schools. I didna think colleges went in for all that crap, or 'philosophy' as they choose to label it in the prospectus. Though I wouldna mind having to be in a tutor group, if Luke were in it with me.

The first day will be the worst. I've no doubt it'll be like being back at Stoneley High again. People thrusting computer print-out timetables into ma hands, an' instructing me to go to certain rooms to which I'll no' know the way. It'll sound like another language, one that nobody has had the grace or common sense to let me in on. Ma own fault really, if I were to face the harsh facts that ma dad's so keen to shove in ma face. I know I should have gone to all the other Open Evenings an' whatever else I missed. There were even mock lessons an' that on offer, but it seemed like a waste o'ma time, at the time. I knew exactly where I was after applying to. Everyone had decided to go to

Maidstone College, an' once Luke decided he was going there too that was ma fate sealed an' sorted. I don't care what it looks like, or how big the refectory is or that they have MTV in there (actually I am a wee bit interested in the MTV deal). What I really care about is that Luke is going to be near to me for at least two more years. I didna even consider ma dad's suggestions about other colleges, an' refused to talk to ma mum about Edinburgh. They didna seem to notice ma heavy an' exaggerated reluctance to discuss this an' carried on anyway.

'But you've no' thought through all the options, Isla. Edinburgh has plenty of colleges that would snap you up with your science grades. Your mum an' I would be happy to move back. Can you no' just think about it the while?'

Ma dad has obviously been informed, by some authority on teenagers, that the best time to lecture your offspring is at Sunday lunch. Maybe it has been scientifically proven that the combination of the soul-destroying day that is Sunday, coupled with the aromatic lure of your regular Sunday lunch an' the hangover from the night before, allows the parent or the hunter to trap their young or prey, secure them firmly to the table, an' proceed to lecture them for the duration of the meal. I think that's why I have such intense indigestion every Sunday, 'cos I have to bolt ma lunch down in order to get out o'there alive, dodging the suggestions and accusations disguised as 'advice' that fly at me across the red wine, the sacrificial blood waiting to be shed.

I know ma dad wants me to think about Edinburgh, 'cos it would give him the excuse he needs to move us back there, now that ma gran's better an' out of hospital. Ma mum however does genuinely believe I'll get a better education up there. She's no' too impressed with the colleges down here – a wee patriot still.

'Isla . . . why no' just look at the prospectus again? You know what the campus is like there an' Laura really loved it. She said the teachers were excellent an' the departments really strong, an' she got two As an' a B in the end.'

Ma mum thinks Laura, ma cousin, is heaven-sent, a superior being designed an' packaged by the angels to show the rest of us how wonderful we could be too, if we could all have angelic aspirations. What ma mum fails to appreciate and acknowledge is that I don't care what grades Laura got at the Edinburgh Academy. These are facts that fail to hold ma interest, beneath the veneer of jealousy that I veil across the whole academic episode which is transmitted down the phone by Auntie Ailsa.

'Laura did sociology, theatre studies an' film studies! O'course she got good grades, she only had to watch a few films, go an' see some plays an' look at some weird people's behaviour. What's that got to do with science an' what I'm after doing?'

I know, I know she had to do more than that but sometimes ma mum is so short-sighted. She knows why I want to stay here, an' I think I know why she wants to go back. I canny help her memories an' I canny change them either. I know they wouldn't stop if we did move back to Edinburgh, Hannah'd be there too. She forgets I have these feelings too an' that I miss her. Still, just because I don't cry doesna mean I feel less, does it?

LUKE

It wasn't a mind-blowingly difficult decision to stay on at college, it was just the geography of it I had to think about – where to actually go and do these A levels or AS things or whatever they're called. The transfer offer put in by my dad was tempting, even if it involved living in dangerously close proximity to the manager, Claire, and her perms and contact lenses which have to be taken in and out and talked about incessantly, then located when she invariably loses them. Again. My dad's flat really is too small – and it's not just his place it's hers as well, so that really closed off that avenue firmly for me. In reality I knew there was no way I would be beholden to her, eating off her beige plates and using her beige bath and having to sit on the same toilet as her. It's juvenile and immature I know, but I don't want to share that kind of close contact with her, ever. Too close for any kind of comfort. Neither do I wish to dwell on the prospect of her arse, which is probably beige too. That can't be a pleasant thought for anyone, my dad included, surely? I have to stop these particular trains of thought before they all pile up and crash.

I don't want to leave my mum now that Matthew's gone to university. She jokes about peace and quiet but I know she's just giving me options and letting me go in order for me to come back. She's got all this American diatribe and psychology that she surrounds herself with and that fills most of our bookcases. Not that I have read any of the books – the covers are enough to put me off with their pictures of calming lakes and ridiculous titles promising tranquillity. I can hear the annoying American accent in the titles, not that I am xenophobic. An excellent word, xenophobia. So I did learn something in English after all. Always useful to have words like that to slip into conversations with adults, who raise their eyebrows and look impressed, I think, unless I have got the wrong meaning.

I don't have anything against Americans though. I only know three – well, not really know, just met once really. On holiday a couple of years ago in Salou, in Spain. The dad was called Ed and he had a loud checked shirt on and things on his feet which he called sneakers, but I could see they were just crap tennis shoes playing at being trainers. The mum didn't have a name – she was called Mom, and she laughed at everything Ed said, which ended up being quite a lot. In a loud, proud, arrogant voice, he informed everyone in the vicinity that we were to come and stay any time we were in the States, which we all silently agreed there and then would be pretty much never. The son was the worst though. He, poor sod, was called Randy and had a baseball cap permanently attached to his head with 'Dodgers' printed on it – or Todgers as Matthew and I liked to call them. The joke was entirely wasted on him. I don't think Americans have quite the same sense of humour as us.

We never saw his hair, or bangs as they called them, which were obviously quite a feature as the family frequently talked about them. Like the Todgers thing with Randy, bangs were in turn lost on me. I never found out what they were or what they looked like. Eventually Matthew took pity on me and informed me in the most sneery manner possible that bangs are a 'fringe'. All those hours of watching *Dawson's Creek* had clearly paid off. And this Randy kid saw absolutely nothing wrong in the name his sneaker-wearing parents had cruelly landed him with. He'd never survive in a school in this country. He'd have to leave, weighed down with all the sex jokes that would have to be made on a regular basis, mostly during the daily registrations. Imagine the teacher saying 'Randy?' and he'd have to answer 'Yes'. There's no way anyone is going to pass up that opportunity, me included.

So my vast knowledge of Americans isn't that vast really. Even so, I do have an idea of what they spout in these philosophy, or is it psychology, books that my mum has, as she often quotes some of their pearls of wisdom at me. Mostly she thinks that if she gives us a 'free rein' and the chance to explore and make our own mistakes then we won't need to rebel and escape. It sort of makes sense and I am definitely in favour of the free rein and making mistakes part, whilst at the same time having my washing done and meals cooked. And though I'd admit it to no one, it will be nice having my mum there as ever, just looking after me now Matthew is at uni. So the offer from Mum has been negotiated, rewritten and finally accepted, and the transfer offer from my dad to Leigh-on-Sea, home of soft furnishings and the unofficial temple of Ikea, rejected.

Isla is delighted and I think it fair to say a little delirious that I am going to Maidstone College. Much kissing and contact of a passionate nature has ensued as a result of my news and this I can confirm is not bad. I don't know how it's all going to work out at college though. Some of me wants us to be this really cool couple and for everyone to see that she is mine and that not only am I wanted but that I am clearly in a relationship, experienced and a man of the world. The other bits of me want to wait to see what it's like when I get there. God, what if . . . I mean . . . maybe Isla and I aren't suited and there's someone else out there waiting for me, not necessarily better, but there, even at college, lurking in my maths class, although in my vast experience of maths students this scenario is not likely.

I am going to do maths, business studies, economics and media studies. The last one is really my favourite and I am looking forward to watching and making lots of films and videos and soundtracks and all of that. The others I just have to do – it's in my contract with the RAF and I like maths really, although no one actually believes me when I tell them and presume I am taking the piss, so I let them. Isla's gutted that we aren't in the same tutor group or any of the same classes, but then I wasn't expecting to see her in economics, seeing as she only just got her C in maths, which seemed to make her day when we went into school for our results. Just as well she got it, otherwise I would have received an earful, in my unrewarded role as her unofficial tutor. We spent the whole of our study leave in May and June ('study leave my arse' said Matthew) fighting over maths revision. I spent all of May trying to get her to master equations and Pythagoras' theorem and Isla, in return and payment in kind, initiated me into the ways of kissing and other methods of seduction throughout the sunny and definitely hot month of June. By July we had both excelled in these art forms, under a system of intensified tutoring. I'd have to say I learn through practical experience and a hands-on approach.

It sounds funny saying 'school' now, really embarrassing. I kind of want to ignore it and pretend I never even went there and that I've always been seventeen (nearly), mature and highly educated in all kinds of subjects, some of which were definitely not taught at school. This is why the whole tutor group thing is going to annoy me when college actually starts. There's no call for it, no need, it's a real waste of my time and theirs. We have to have tutorials every Thursday morning. Typically this coincides with the one day I have no lessons. There is no way I am going to get up and come into college purely to look at my tutor for an hour and listen to him impress us with his cool and laid-back attitudes to life. We are supposed to follow a syllabus with the topics we have to 'discuss'. No one ever sticks to any of this until it's university applying time, according to the lord of the higher education system that is my brother, who has, annoyingly, been there and done it all before me. I still want someone to explain what this syllabus is going to do for me and why I need a tutor at all. So far no one's given me a good explanation, and that includes Mr Davis, or 'Jim' as he asked us to call him on the Open Day. Jim, my new tutor. Great.

ISLA

I didna think it would all happen quite so quickly. Year 11 didna seem to be a full year – it felt as if we'd only got bits of it, hardly spent any time in school, an' I kinda wanted ma money back. First off we were booted out on work experience, an' then loaded with timetables for our mock exams, an' then escorted off the premises for study leave. We had so many different exams that it took me nearly half an hour to work the timetable out, an' I wasna being lazy, I was properly confused. It was so complicated, with all these letters an' Option groups an' English sets an' all of that.

It was a wee bit frightening getting the mock exam results, 'cos I had thought the exams were quite easy but Andrew James told me that meant that I had screwed up, the sod. I didna care too much about things like French an' geography but I was bitter concerned an' angry about maths, no' so much that I canny do it but that I have to have it. I can remember ma careers interview that I had to wait ages for. It was held in the careers library, which is just a wee dark cupboard room that has fallen off the library room over the years an' no one has bothered to join them back together.

'Come in.' A warm welcome from the careers adviser, whose name no one ever quite remembered, but it didna matter 'cos anyone's name in school you didna know you could call 'Miss' or 'Sir' an' you'd be grand an' in no bother.

'Right then . . . um . . . ' All that worry an' she couldna remember my name either. I supplied her with it, wrapping it in an air of injustice and haughtiness that she, a teacher, could have forgotten ma name.

'OK, so . . . what are your plans for when you leave school?' Now this seemed to me to be a stupid question, as surely the reason I was there was for her to give me some plans with which to leave school, or had I got it all wrong?

'Umm . . . I dunno.' I couldna seem to be very excited or full of ideas. This was really hard an' embarrassing. I had turned into a monosyllabic teenage boy. I think she might have seen one or two of these kinds o'creatures afore though as she wasna insulted by ma lack of sparkle.

'Right. OK. Well, let's see – are you planning on going to college? Yes? Good. OK, we're getting somewhere now . . . '

Several minutes later she had got out of me that I had gone to hospital, not to be ill but on work experience, an' that I liked science an' people (although this was stretching the truth a wee bit). Once she'd latched on to the hospital bit there was no stopping her. I was to become a nurse, of course! The only thing that stopped her from making me a doctor there an' then were ma predicted results. Namely ma maths.

'Oh God . . . goodness, I mean. You will need to sort this out if you are planning on being a nurse, won't you? Now then, you need a C, so you're going to have to move up two grades, aren't you? An E . . . well, it is possible, isn't it? You know you will need your maths for any job you want to do these days . . . '

After she had killed an' crushed me with what has to be the most annoying reminder in the history of ma life I left the room like a girl possessed. I had to get a C in maths if I were to become a nurse, something I was clearly destined to be. I mean, she'd just told me I was going to be a nurse, 'cos I loved people an' hospitals as she'd helpfully pointed out. I had to get ma maths. So I employed Luke in ma mad revision panic, an' in other pursuits too, of course.

Our study leave was spent outside on Luke's back lawn, which is a wee bit small – there's only room for two an' a couple of maths textbooks, which make good pillows for the head there. I had to put them to good use after going to the effort of persuading the maths teacher to give me another set, ma third in total. I did open them to test maself on the past papers, though it was much easier when I realised the answers were all worked out for you an' written in the back of the book by some wee kind person. Once I had the answers I could work out how to do the bloody things. Luke failed to see the logic in this, but I proved him wrong (only just though).

The official last day at school was weird an' there were hugs an' tears, though not from the girls obviously. Our form tutor Miss Hughes took lots of photos of us, whilst she kept saying the same things over an' over about how quickly the year had all gone an' that we would always be her favourite tutor group. Her only one, really, as she's leaving school an' teaching altogether, to get married. I think we tired her out, she's probably ready to relax an' have a wee bairn an' be a mum instead now. She cried a wee bit when we gave her a new watch as a leaving present, which was of course banshee-girl Georgia Hopkins's idea. Even Andrew James put a quid in for it. I don't think I've ever seen him pay for anything himself before, at least nothing legal.

I'd to babysit the day the results came out an' it felt weird with a wee bairn crying on ma hip as I tried to open ma brown envelope to see if I'd freed maself from further maths torture, which thank God I had, scraping ma C with the help of Luke. I didna even notice the rest o'ma grades until I'd checked ma maths a couple o'times, just to make sure I wasna hallucinating or too hung over to see sense. I had an A for drama which I was really wanting an' two As for ma sciences, then the rest were all OK, except for design an' French, two wee Es making a mess of ma list and certificates, but I didna care. I really didna. I know people say that all the time, that they don't care what they get, an' you can tell they don't mean it as they grit their teeth an' toss their heads an' look away. I honestly did mean it though – I didn't care about design or French, most of which I had spent on ma own, removed from the lessons as I caused too much of a disturbance an' disruption there.

I actually quite liked turning up at school with a baby an' watching Mr Bourgoine's face get longer an' longer with his tired mouth flapping open as Luke kissed me when I told him about ma C. Perfect timing. I told him just as Mr Bourgoine was watching us. For some reason I hoped he thought that the bairn was ours, I don't really know why.

It was weird going back to school in jeans an' a T-shirt when it wasna a non-uniform day. I felt strange an' grown-up, an' even the teachers were different, either taking the 'matey' approach or the 'deeply concerned about your future' tone, matched with a bowing of the head and the creased brow, crippled by the seriousness of it all. Then there were those who were clearly just glad to get rid of us.

Practically all of us had a leaver's book, which in truth were just your basic notebooks, cute for the lasses and plain for the lads. Mine, ma dad's contribution from the shop, had wee blue elephants at the bottom of each page. You wanted everyone to sign yours, and the longer and funnier the note, the higher up in the popularity stakes you rose. It was all a bit stupid an' vain, like you were never gonny clap eyes on any of them again, which for some was true I suppose – Andrew James for example. He swore all

26

over two pages of ma elephant book. Lots of it was artificial though, hugging an' talking to people you've ignored the whole year or who have ignored you, an' there was a desperate feeling in ma stomach of something big coming to a depressing end. Luke didna sign ma book, he said there was no need for him to as we'd be going to Newquay in a couple o'days an' o'course I would be seeing him all over the summer an' then at college. I still wanted him to write something, something I could keep for ever, just in case.

LUKE

I wanted to go surfing and to the beach and have a holiday, but without Matthew it would be weird and I didn't want to experience only-child syndrome and be a gooseberry with Dad and Claire. The whole holiday thing came up when I was staying with them for the weekend, forced to by Matthew, of course – his last performance as Peace Keeper and UN Ambassador for our family. What a family. Dad, sons, mum, step-mum, step-grandparents, step-cousins etc. Why 'step' I don't know – maybe it means 'half' or 'nearly there, one more step'.

The dictionary definition for step is 'lift and set foot down/stepping in time with others/conform-ing/watch one's step/related by re-marriage of a par-ent/intervene'. Well, the last one is about right. Claire had intervened in our family. If she hadn't come to work for Dad then none of this would have happened. She must have known he was married – he had a huge gold band on his finger, pictures on his desk and a marriage certificate. But no, that didn't stop them. I asked him about it once – why they did it, to my mum, to us. He said they fell in love! At his age! He was supposed to be in love with my mum. They must have been in love once.

No matter how many times I think about it I don't get what happened. I've seen the photos of their wedding day, our birthdays, parties, holidays, Christmases. They look so normal and happy, and now those photos seem like a lie 'cos he was never happy with us and had to go and find someone else – her. So when he left I cut him out of my photos, ones I'd taken with my little Fisher Price camera, and now I wish I hadn't 'cos it's embarrassing to see how much I cared when he went.

Anyway I will never get used to her or pretend that we are now related just because my dad married her. She is nothing to me, and no matter how much Matthew tries to pretend that it will be OK and that we will get on and I will be adult about it one day, I know I never will. My mum isn't making us pretend that some other man is our father or that it's right to call him Step-Dad. I hate it when Dad comes to parents' evenings with Claire and they bump into my mum and the teacher tries to work out who is who and mistakes Claire for my mum! It disgusts me. Why don't they stop flaunting it and think of her? Claire is so selfish. She couldn't get her own man so she had to steal my dad and his family. Well, no matter how many cans of Fosters she gives me or cinema tickets or other freebies from her pathetic mates in the 'industry', she won't buy my affection and I will never like her.

So I tell them straight when they ask if I would like to go on holiday to Newquay with them, knowing Mum can't afford to take us anywhere.

'Yeah thanks, but I don't think so. I've got plans here really and I said I'd help Matthew with Ripper's car, so cheers and that. I'll look after the flat if you want?' I think the last offer is a stroke of genius and make sure it sounds casual, like I am doing them a favour. I hope I have managed to say no without sounding too rude, 'cos in a way I'd quite like to go but not . . . well, not on my own with them, plus I like the idea of having their flat to myself and Isla.

'Do you really think I'd let you look after the flat? No way mate!' Apparently, my dad doesn't trust me. I am getting ready to be insulted and do my wounded deer impression when Claire stops me, launching her red-nailed hand on to my dad's arm. *My* dad's arm.

'Darling, why don't we suggest to Luke what we were . . . discussing before?' Claire doesn't have conversations or talk to people, she discusses or debates issues, normally winning. Well, she isn't going to win this one. Whatever creepy little scenario she has been discussing with my dad she can forget it. I am not going to be manipulated by her long scarlet talons, even if my dad is.

'Do you think so, love? Luke, how would you feel about inviting Isla along with us to Newquay? The cottage has plenty of room and if her parents agree, then it's fine with us.'

As my dad is suggesting these results of their discussion, Claire is observing me with a look that says it all. Mostly how brilliant she is, devising such a winning suggestion, and how cool she is to invite her stepson's girlfriend on holiday. My dad seems to think he has just offered me several Christmas and birthday presents rolled into one, which in a way he has, but I have my pride and dignity to think of.

'I'll think about it . . . and let you know, yeah?' It is meant to be a business-like conclusion to our discussion meeting, which seems to be the tone I try to take whenever talking to Claire. I think it comes out more like a question 'cos my dad comes back with an answer.

'Sure, Luke. Have a chat to Isla and see what she thinks. No rush, as it's booked anyway. Give us a ring and let us know.'

Then that is the end. I have to walk very slowly to the station, in case of eyes spying through the window of the flat – a riverside loft apartment, of course. This mature, concentrated reaction lasts until I am safely on the train, then I let out a big sigh and a smile that has been bursting to dance all over my face. Yes! I am going on holiday with my girlfriend to Newquay, in a cottage, on our own. Well, apart from Dad and Claire, but maybe I can put up with her for a week or two if it means Isla and I can be by ourselves.

ISLA

I'd never been to Newquay before – the one in Cornwall, not the one in Wales. In fact I didna know there were two places by the same name until ma dad informed me. I think it was his way of stalling for time when I told him Luke had asked me to go with him, for a whole two weeks, to Newquay. Though it was Luke's dad really who was after asking me, as it's his cottage – his an' Claire's, the stepmother from hell according to Luke. He reckons she makes the wicked stepmothers in fairy tales look just that, as if they're literally from fairy tales and harmless in comparison. I asked him to identify Claire's exact crime and list the atrocities she's committed against him. He got really huffy an' sighed an' rolled his eyes at me, like I'd just asked him how to work out some awful equation or name the capital of Greenland.

So ma dad was trying to control his spluttering, whilst looking from ma mum to me to the floor, presumably searching for a good reason to say no to ma reasonable request. I had done ma best no' to sound like I were asking permission or requesting anything. I had wanted to be able to go into the lounge an' say 'Luke's asked me to go to Newquay with him and I've said yes'. Unfortunately, I missed out the crucial ending in which I inform ma dad, mid smug grin, that I have already said yes. I must have run out of breath there, that or guts. Ma mum sat down on the sofa, an' arranged her face into a thoughtful expression, creating the 'calm' look that I had witnessed frequently over the years at ma requests, which have lately turned into whiny, high-pitched demands, all still meeting with the same calm face.

Ma dad didna even attempt this expression. His face was screwed up an' contorted, an' showed seven shades of panic, his hair bouncing as his head swung from side to side, from ma mum to me, then back again, wordless, clueless.

'Oh.'

Now this were no' an interested 'Oh', perhaps leading on to the famous an' much overused phrase of 'We'll see'. 'We'll see' normally meant 'no' until ma mum had a chance to exercise her diplomatic skills, when she would gently remind ma dad that we no longer live in caves an' that women have actually had the vote for some time now. Ma dad's 'Oh' was neatly followed by ma mum's string of questions, uttered slowly and professionally, like she were a newsreader working from her autocue.

'Who will be going?'

Easy one, this. Two adults. I should be safe enough here.

'Luke's dad and . . . Claire.' I really emphasised the Claire addition as she is another adult an' really sensible. I looked at ma mum's face . . . passed! Next . . .

'Where will you be staying?'

Now this one was loaded an' labelled 'Handle with care'. It didna just mean what form of accommodation, but what were the sleeping arrangements? I noted that the word 'sleeping' had been politely removed so as not to cause offence to the innocent. I think I was supposed to be the innocent. Ma mum had substituted the offensive verb with 'staying'. Very clever.

'In their cottage. It's got loads of space, an' rooms an' stuff.' I didna actually know this for sure. I'd no' seen the place or a photo or anything, an' I was hardly going to ask Luke how many bedrooms it had, for fear of sounding like, well . . . like ma mum. So I hadna. I was hoping the 'stuff' I added on to the end of my sentence would move us neatly on to the next line of questioning. No such luck.

'How many bedrooms does it have?'

Shit. No covering up or politeness or euphemisms here. Straight out with it. Now, improvise, lie or tell it straight? Improvising seemed the best option.

'Three.' Short an' sweet an' to the point. No ums or ers here.

'How long would you be going for?'

I didna like the sound of the word 'would'. It was too hypothetical for me. I wanted her to use the word 'will'. How long *will* you be going for?

'Only two weeks – well, twelve nights really, once we've driven down . . . ' It was here, criminally early in the proceedings, that a fatal mistake was made. I had used the word 'nights'. It was clearly too much for ma dad, who then collapsed, terminating the discussion/interrogation with the classic . . .

'We'll see.'

At ma age, nearly seventeen (the nearly part having more kudos than 'sixteen and five months'), I was none too happy with the parental response. Ma dad cut up the conversation by leaving the room with a snippy nod of the head, clearly reeling with all kinds of scenarios about the cottage, which was obviously the 'den of iniquity', whatever that means. I heard him call it that later as I eavesdropped on their post-interrogation negotiations, which took place in the boardroom, more commonly known as the kitchen. They always make their decisions in there, door firm-ly closed to me an' Hannah. We used to press up against it when we were little, with a glass to our ear, our spying skills cheaply borrowed from James Bond films. We would try an' make out the words under-neath the clattering of plates an' the chink of glasses, as they washed up noisily to cover their tracks.

I wished Hannah were around, so I wouldna feel so childish eavesdropping on ma own – shameful at ma age really. I hoped ma mum would turn the 'We'll see' into a 'Yes!' whilst she softened ma dad's prehistoric resolve over the soap suds.

LUKE

A fortnight is fourteen days, there's twenty-four hours in a day, that's 24 x 14, which is 336 hours. Lots of girls at school used to say that, 'Twenty-four-seven', as in 'He's with me, like, twenty-four-seven, yeah?' They'd talk about their boyfriends, always older and preferably with a car, normally an old Escort or Vauxhall. They'd twiddle their cheap gold rings, signs of possession, and moan about twenty-four-seven loving and their relationship commitments, which probably only lasted one set of twenty-four-seven.

There's sixty minutes in an hour, so 336 x 60 is a lot of time. I decided I didn't want to work out the minutes and seconds part as I felt I had made my point and didn't want to fall into the trap of speaking in these terms and ending my sentences with 'yeah' or 'like' with my voice rising to a challenge at the end. I mean, there was no denying Isla and I'd have dangerous amounts of time together alone in Newquay. Isla didn't really need this mathematical form of persuasion. Her dad, however, needed as much persuasion as possible. I knew he didn't trust me. I know he still doesn't and that I am 'that Luke', though that's fine by me 'cos he's 'your father' or 'that twat' depending on whose company I am in, though mostly I keep the last phrase to myself, something to make me smile as I utter it aloud in my head.

I want to have time alone with her, to stay in my dad's cottage and go to the beach and show her all the best bits of Newquay, but I'm sort of scared, I think. If my dad just lets us get on with it, which he will as he'll be busy keeping Claire happy, then Isla and I can do what we want and we've never been able to do that before. I mean, I will have to make the decisions as to what happens. Presumably there'll be sun, sand and, well, sex. Let's face it, two nearly-seventeen-year-olds in love, well in lust anyway, and a cottage to ourselves – we'd be mad not to take advantage, wouldn't we?

Even my mum seems to expect it – she gave me the whole 'condoms and sensible sex' talk. Sensible sex? Who has sensible sex? Whatever it is it doesn't sound like much fun. I want to have unsensible, fun sex and I am sure Isla wants the same. I've been told to take precautions by my mum and then Matthew put a pack of Durex in my rucksack so I guess it's all sorted then –

off for two weeks of sex, with the approval of the family. Weird or what. It almost puts me off. Almost.

God, what if I'm crap and don't know how to do it properly? I mean obviously I've had sex before, at least I think I have. We did the basics but, well, it didn't feel like what everyone talks about. The earth didn't move, I didn't scream her name over and over and she didn't drag her fingernails down my back, which does look painful admittedly. So maybe we didn't do it right. I wish there were someone who would tell you what it's really honestly like – the real sex, teenage sex, not some awful film with Brad Pitt smarming over some stick-insect model who is climbing the walls with passion and luuuurrrrve for Brad. It doesn't work like that, does it?

Try having sex in a single bed, Pitt! Sex in your girl-friend's bedroom while her parents are out, but could be home any moment and come barging in, doesn't really create the romantic candle-lit atmosphere you want, does it! No wonder we both felt so strange. It was almost a race to get on with it and get it done, ticked that one off, lost my virginity, as if it were a dreadful curse hanging over me, a social stigma, particularly since most of the blokes in my year claim to have lost it when they were thirteen to some twenty-six-year-old Brazilian model on holiday! Of course I agreed that I too had lost it before I had even reached double figures. I don't think any of us believed each other, but you have to say it, don't you?

So I'd finally done it, last month, though it was not really very good, I have to admit. We haven't had the opportunity again, though we haven't really tried very hard to create one. So the pressure is now on! Newquay will be the BIG SEDUCTION! The holiday of love and romance, and I will make sure I get it right this time. Brad Pitt move over, there's a new player in town.

That's if it's OK with Mr Kelman, and the wrath of the father! I mean he couldn't exactly say no, could he? We're both sixteen, nearly seventeen. Legally we could get married, if we wanted to I mean, not that we do as the prospect of getting married right now would bloody terrify me. In fact getting married full stop terrifies me and every living male if he's telling the truth. This of course is something he would never do in the company of his girlfriend; tell the truth that is, or at least not regarding the minefield that is marriage. I think proposing, vows, flowers, presents, rings and all that shit is taking things a little too far for just a week or two in Newquay. There are certain lengths

I would go to for Isla and, like the Milk Tray man, I would valiantly climb many a mountain, but to take the holy sacrament of marriage for a fortnight in Cornwall is a length too far. Even if the lady does love Milk Tray, she can have a Mars bar instead.

ISLA

Newquay was lovely – the place, that is. It was amazing. Totally beautiful, dream-like almost. I've never been anywhere so pretty, with such dramatic scenery, that is actually warm and not sub-zero like Scotland. I even came home a sort of pink-white-red colour. Scots start off blue, with veins that look like an Ordnance Survey map, then after several hours of burning an' frying ourselves in the midday heat we turn a lovely proud shade of white, followed by a shade of pink, if we're lucky. I was this fortunate shade of pink by the end of the first week, an' with a careful application of ma mum's expensive 'DO NOT TOUCH FOR FEAR OF YOUR OWN LIFE!' fake tan I managed to develop a convincing glow of marbled orange. My, how I love being a Celt! The orange did blend in particularly well with ma freckles though, so I couldna complain too much, an' once the smell had died down no one would ever be able to tell.

We got to Cornwall in about four hours, which did

include two stops, one for Claire to check she had packed her contact lens solution an' another for Claire to check she had packed her contact lens case. Luke was ready to jump out of the car an' hitch back home at this point but I kindly diverted his attention with the map so we could plan which beach we would hit first the next day. Luke wanted to learn how to surf an' I had promised him I would give it a go too.

I knew I'd be crap as I am useless at that sort of thing. We went ice-skating once and ma arse was covered in multi-coloured bruises in a matter of minutes. I canny rollerblade either, all the cool sporty stuff is just a recipe for disaster when it comes to me an' ma legs. They seem purposefully to ignore all the messages ma brain is screaming at them as we approach a tree or lamppost at full speed. So I normally tend to try an' stay clear of that kind of thing, but I was determined to give surfing a go for Luke. He had put so much time an' effort into thinking about this holiday, our first away together, that I couldna let him down at the first hurdle. He was so excited an' so was I but I was nervous too.

I didna know why I was nervous. I had met his dad, Tom, and Claire a couple of times and they had come over to ma parents' at ma dad's insistence, so they could get to know the people who were taking me away to the 'den of iniquity'. O'course once my dad had met Claire he changed his mind. You could never accuse her of being anything other than sensible, efficient, practical and, well, boring really. She's like an adult Girl Guide or something. So once Dad had met her an' saw the company I would be in, he reluctantly grumbled 'Yes' to ma request an' off we went.

The journey wasna too bad, once we'd stopped stopping. Luke an' I sat in the back an' behaved like a couple of school kids, it's fair to say. Within the first two hours we'd eaten all our sweets an' chocolate, read each other's magazines (mine *Cosmo* an' his *Loaded*), swapped mini discs, an' run out of things to say. So we began to eavesdrop on his dad an' Claire, to see if they would let slip anything about the baby. Luke is convinced Claire is secretly pregnant, or is about to become so. It's his greatest fear. I can understand why, but at the same time I would love another brother or sister. He says that's because I lost Hannah. Apparently I wouldna feel that way if ma mum an' dad got divorced an' moved on to new partners.

Anyway, Tom and Claire weren't talking about anything interesting, just boring current affairs shite, news an' politics an' that, which I had no interest in, and neither did Luke, although he liked to pretend he did, asking me what I thought about the crisis in Afghanistan, trying to catch me out. I knew about that, I mean how could you not? It's just I don't know all the wee men's names, or which country they are president of.

When we finally got there I was so excited. The cottage was gorgeous. It had roses surrounding the door frame, potted plants all along the front wall. The curtains were held back with little ties, the huge table in the kitchen was an antique scrubbed pine one, with eight chairs sat round it, the beds were huge with pine bed-heads an' sweet little bedside tables. There were fresh flowers in every room an' I was sure I could smell bread baking in the Aga. It was almost too much! I couldn't help asking how come there were flowers everywhere when I knew Tom and Claire hadn't been down since Easter.

'We have a lady who comes in and does for us, don't we darling?' Claire answered before Luke's dad could get a word in. She seemed to do that, to answer for him. I think she likes being in charge. I wondered what the woman who 'does' for them actually does. I guessed she was their cleaning lady but Claire couldn't bring herself to say that – she could be a bit funny sometimes about things like that.

Once we'd got everything in from the car, Claire and Tom went off to their room to unpack, which left Luke and me in the hallway with our bags an' two bedrooms to choose from. I didna know if we were meant to have a room together or one each – Claire and Tom hadn't said anything. I looked at Luke an' he was no help, I couldna read his face, so I took a deep breath and moved towards the prettiest bedroom. Both rooms had double beds but this one looked more feminine an' if I were supposed to have a room on ma own I thought this would be it. I turned round to ask Luke what he thought an' he scowled at me, muttering, 'Fine, if that's what you want,' and slammed off into the bedroom opposite.

I had messed up. He obviously thought that I wanted to be on ma own. God, I wish we were clear and simple like Claire an' Tom – they knew what they wanted an' said so. Luke an' I are so indecisive around one another an' so confused. We've slept together loads of times and actually had sex a couple of times but I wasna to know that meant we were to share a bedroom – we've never done that. Secretly I am glad he's stormed off, 'cos I'm no' sure about the whole sex thing yet, let alone him seeing me in the morning without ma make-up an' hair done!

So I was sat on the squashy bed on ma own. The first day an' already it was all ruined. Might as well go home, except I couldn't, could I? I was in the vulnerable position of no' being able to drive home, or get to a train station to get home, an' I couldna tell Tom or Claire as they would think I were an immature, spoilt little madam if I went an' told them Luke an' I had fallen out already an' that I wanted to go home. Ma dad would say 'I told you so and it serves you right' if I rang him up. Actually he probably wouldna, but I felt stupid an' foolish an' very alone.

I didna know what to do. Was I over-reacting? Had we broken up now? Were we all right? I felt like ending the whole thing an' starting again, elsewhere, far away from Luke, Maidstone an' college. Maybe I shouldha thought more carefully about ma future an' looked at other colleges an' no' just chosen Maidstone 'cos Luke was going there.

I felt like such a sheep, just following people around ma whole life an' doing what they say an' what they want. Maybe I didn't want to be a nurse any more. Maybe science isn't everything an' there are other courses I might like to do. Maybe there are better colleges out there an' I should go to one all on ma own.

OK, maybe no' the last bit as that would be too scary, but I think I might have made a mistake with ma AS options. I didna even look at the other choices. I just went for science as that's what everyone had decided I should do.

Our argument, or rather another wee misunderstanding, made me think about other stuff that I wouldn't think about normally.

I wish I were twenty-five or something, living in a loft apartment with a good job, friends and money, and were allowed to do exactly what I liked and make ma own decisions without having to check with anyone else.

I wish I were more worldly wise.

LUKE

I am so pissed off and wish I had never bothered with the whole thing. God! I go to the effort of inviting her down here to spend time with me and she goes off and picks the girly, flowery bedroom and shuts the door. I mean what kind of a message is that? I feel such a fool. I am so angry with her. I have never felt like this before. Why do I bother? She is such hard work. If it were anyone else I would have split up with them by now, dumped them, got rid of them and moved on, but somehow I can't. It's like I have invested so much time in her and gone through so much that to end it now would be like a waste, plus when its good it is aaaaaamazing and well worth the effort.

I am so confused. I will never understand women and why we are so attracted to them, they are so weird and different to us, almost alien, another species. Why do they get in such moods and cry and get so upset about the smallest thing and go on about it even when it's well over and you've moved on, except they haven't and it's ammunition for a later date when you annoy them about something else? I reckon it's put in the filing cabinet labelled 'Get him back later'. Five weeks on when you are having a discussion over something else, totally unrelated, they will mentally fling open the cabinet, flick through the files and find their evidence which proves that once, a long time ago, you were wrong and therefore will now lose this argument and any others in the future. They are so infuriating. Why can't they be as laid back as us and just go with the flow a bit more? But no! They have to remember everything you ever did and never forget it or let you forget it either. Better memories than elephants, women, not that I am comparing Isla to an elephant as I value my young life too much for that.

Then there's the unspoken argument that couples have in public, like in a shopping centre, when you can tell the woman wants a major scene with the man but there are too many people around, and you can see her hissing at him out of the corner of her mouth, then looking up and smiling at everyone pretending that everything is fine.

Then there is the LOOK! You know, the kind women give men, mums give kids and teachers give their students. Like on the way down to Newquay Claire was really annoying me and I couldn't help letting out the occasional sigh and huff a little bit in the back seat when we'd had to stop for the third time and I had lost the will to live. I felt like taking my dad to one side and explaining that anyone who was that obsessed with their contact lenses was a sad case and really ought to get out more. Why couldn't he have found a normal woman? Instead of a permed blinking owl who, let's face it, wears fake nails. So Isla kept giving me the LOOK.

The look that says I will boil you alive and hang you by your bits if you don't shut up/behave/calm down. They then hold this stare longer than is humanly possible, making you look away at the last moment, catching their victorious facial expression before you cave in and agree to meet their demands. The bullies. Women, they always win and they are always right somehow. I am not sure how they manage it.

It'd be so much easier if I were gay – not that I am, of course. I don't actually mean it about the gay thing – it's probably just as hard, 'cos not only would you have the whole do they fancy me thing but also are they even batting for my side, are they actually gay?

Anyway, I've got to sort all this out. Even my dad is having a better relationship than me, though it's all right for him – he is married and sorted. It seems so much easier when you are older, less worry and nerves about the whole thing – it seems to be easier to talk to one another. I am embarrassed even to mention our 'relationship' to Isla for fear of sounding like an idiot masquerading as an adult. We never talk about 'us', we just get on with it, have a row, ignore each other, make up and show everyone and ourselves how perfect we are by kissing, holding hands, hugging lots, going out, giving each other thoughtful presents, having anniversaries of the month we first met/went out on a date/kissed/had a meal together – all the usual stuff, until we end up having another tiff. It's an endless circle but I do think I love her, we never split up properly. Maybe we should.

I think I'll go for a walk and get out of the house, leave her to stew for a bit and wonder where I am and hopefully come looking for me.

ISLA

I had to get out, go for a walk, clear ma head. I'd always fancied charging over the Cornish coast and rampaging along the cliff face, rain lashing into ma face, hair blowing around wildly, me swearing an' cursing men or whatever had annoyed me, most likely life in general. Like Cathy from *Wuthering Heights*, out on the moors, or a heroine from a Daphne Du Maurier novel, very Cornish an' very suitable. After all, I was going to do English literature for AS.

But there was no pelting rain or howling wind to be had an' I had had yet another disastrous hair cut three days before. As it was the summer I'd thought the Meg Ryan haircut would be appropriate. Will I never learn? Looking like a refugee fluffy chick with barely a hair on ma head was no' a winning look for the traditional lovestruck heroine but I'd have to make do. The gleaming sunlight in ma eyes wasn't really part of ma vision either but it looked like I'd have to live with that too.

So, armed with suntan lotion (factor 30 a prerequisite for a fair-skinned Celt), a book (you never know, I might get bored with torturing ma soul) an' ma shades (as even the traditional heroine wants to look cool), I set off on ma expedition. I walked down the steep sandy path along the side of the cottage an' began ma adventure. I don't really know what I was expecting, but the woodlands I walked through literally made me gasp – I felt like I was in a film, like the whole of the forest path an' the coast I could see peeking through were laid out for me.

There was no one anywhere to be seen, which was what I wanted, but it was still a wee bit creepy. I mean, what if someone were following me or going to attack me? There would be no one to help me. I didn't have ma mobile on me, stupid I know but I forgot to charge it. I calmed maself down an' looked around me at all the greenery, inhaled the fresh air deep into ma lungs an' felt maself relaxing and actually enjoying maself. This was good. It was peaceful, healthy an' free from anyone asking anything of me, or even knowing where I was. Total freedom for a wee while.

I walked for miles, must have been at least three, an' eventually came out of the woods, on to a beach. This was no ordinary beach – it was a wee secluded one, a bay in a triangular shape, with the bluest water I have ever seen. It didna look real, almost a painting-by-numbers manufactured colour, like an altered photo. I wished I had a camera so I could prove it existed. There was no one in the water and no one on the sand. This was more like it. I could sit and think and calm down in the sun, before eventually returning to the house. I had left ma watch in ma room as I didna want to know what time it was. I wanted Luke to worry about me an' come an' find me. It would be light for ages yet, so I was safe.

I sat down on the sand an' felt very warm, calm an' almost happy. If only me and Luke could stop bickering all the time, like kids. We were supposed to be on holiday for God's sake. It didn't help that he hated Claire an' that he had all these feelings going on with his dad. He shouldn't take them out on me though.

As for the whole bedroom thing, I couldna work out if that was the major problem or if that was just another thing annoying him. He had been really moody lately an' no' so much fun. He kept mentioning the RAF an' college an' his plans but his heart didn't seem to be in them. Maybe he was doing as he was told, or doing what he thought he should, like me.

The whole sex thing has me confused. I mean, I want to do it, but when we go to do it or could do it, like at a party, when clothing is going to have to come off an' we are going to have to deal with the totally embarrassing issue that is the condom, it just seems easier to say no an' chicken out. Even though I know that'll get Luke all moody, an' that I should have said 'no' earlier on, I can't seem to speak up. It's like I am suddenly mute. I find the whole thing really weird an' awkward an' I hate talking about it with Luke.

It's all right joking with mates an' laughing an' putting on a show like I know loads an' am really experienced just 'cos Luke an' I have been going out for nearly two years, but I am no' experienced at all. Neither of us is experienced an' that makes it all worse. It's getting in the way now. I should be dying to get him on ma own, an' jump on to any free bed at a party, but I don't want to, so we don't.

I fancy him an' I want to kiss him, want him to touch me, to make love to me. If I were ever to say these words to him, 'make love', sounding like some porn star, I'm sure he'd laugh, but I don't know what I am doing. I have never even kissed anyone other than him, let alone had sex with anyone else. I think he is much more experienced than me an' I just canny bring any of this up, so I just sit there an' say nothing an' let him get cross with me an' pull his trousers back on an' watch him try an' smile at me like it's all OK an' no bother to him.

We both keep pretending we're fine, an' giving each other weak smiles, but then we end up taking it out on each other later on over something tiny that doesn't really annoy us. What we're really annoyed about is the other thing, the thing we can't talk about, but we have to get the anger out somehow.

I know now he wanted me to share a room with him, that he was excited about it, looking forward to being a proper couple, an' I misunderstood him, an' now I have really annoyed him, but he doesn't understand me. AAAAAARRRGGH!

LUKE

Well, I can't see Isla anywhere. She probably doesn't want me to find her. It's half six already, we should be getting ready to go out and have a night out in Newquay, but instead I am sat on the beach throwing stones into the sea, skimming them really badly. I wish I could talk to her about this, but it's so difficult. Whenever I try and bring it up she becomes mute girl and for once is silent. I wish I had the words, or the moves, or whatever it is she wants from me. I am trying so hard not to be some lecherous boyfriend after only one thing, but suddenly this has become so huge and is affecting everything.

Why does sex matter so much? There was a time when I didn't even know about it, its very existence was a mystery to me. There was Matthew and my mum and dad and me and we had all just arrived on the earth and were linked in some way which was very nice, but that was it. The concept of sex was a foreign one until one day at primary school Danny

Drummond and Jason Hassel called me over to look at some pictures in the book they were huddled over in the library. As we were doing a nature project on tadpoles I presumed it was a picture of some frogs. Wrong!

It was a book on reproduction and what they showed me continued to haunt me for years. At eight years old I was not ready for a picture of a man and woman procreating, especially when they informed me 'That's what your mum and dad do every day, in fact that is your mum and dad, eeeerrrrrrrrrrr! Luke's mum and dad do it!!!' This was followed by hysterical laughter and most of the class peering at the book of 'my parents' doing it until Mrs Nightingale came over and hit the boys lightly over the head with the book and dragged us back to the nature pond. No wonder I am having problems now. I should go on *Oprah* for counselling.

Isla and I just don't seem to be able to talk about sex. The more time goes on the worse it gets, until now we've got to the stage where we hardly even try any more to sort it out – it's easier left unsaid. It can't go on. We're sixteen, we are allowed to have sex, we should be having the time of our lives, so why aren't we?

Right. This can't go on, I'm going to find her and sort it out. It's that simple, isn't it? When I find her I am going to apologise and explain what I want and why I wanted to share a room. I was so excited about this holiday and it feels spoilt now but there's still a chance if I apologise. Maybe if we go to the pub and have a few drinks and get a bit pissed she will talk to me. A few drinks loosens the old tongue, gets her a bit chatty – s'pose it does that to all of us.

Isla can be so odd. Sometimes she seems so confident and chatty and flirty and in control and at other times she's like this little kid who knows nothing and is scared of everyone, mostly of me. I think she thinks I am this super stud who has had loads of girlfriends and am MR LOVER LOVER like in the Shaggy song. Well, I am not. Maybe if I told her that, despite the fact that it will make me look like an arse, she might feel better. I wish I had someone to talk this through with. I almost wish Matthew were here. Even though he'd take the piss and make me feel about ten years old, at least he could guess what the matter was and give me some pearls of wisdom from his archives of love. He has had a serious amount of 'ladies', as he calls them, jammy sod. I'd settle for one. I certainly don't want words of advice from my dad. He tried to have a 'chat' with me by the back door as I went to find Isla. He said he'd overheard us arguing. I told him we were not arguing, we were 'discussing things'. Admittedly I said the last bit in a sneery voice which I thought sounded remarkably like Claire's. I don't know whether my dad got it but he looked really cross.

'What is your problem, Luke? We have done everything to get you down here, invited your girlfriend along, driven you down to Cornwall and you still behave like a spoilt brat!'

Now he was right in part. I know I have been a pain but I cannot stop myself, whenever I come into contact with Claire I revert to a 13-year-old boy, acting spoilt, grumpy, putting on a major strop display. I could not stop myself even if I wanted to. I have been all over the place lately, not knowing what's going on, what I want to do, where I want to go. I don't know what's the matter with me. I keep spoiling things, on purpose. I feel like crying, but then boys don't cry, do they? We just get on with it. I have to find Isla and sort this out before I ruin the whole holiday.

ISLA

I felt as if I had lost fifteen stone an' were light, free and airy. I had no idea of the sheer weight of the worry I had been carrying around with me. Amazing that it could all just disappear in one fell swoop. I was officially a woman. How it happened I don't really know, but I am glad it did. I finally feel like I understand all the books, magazines and conversations I have always felt so removed from.

Yipeeee! Finally I had done it, an' done it properly. I had had sex, made love, shagged, got it on – whatever you want to call it, we had done it! An' it felt like the best secret in the world ever an' it was wonderful! Every cliché you could think of couldn't start to describe it. I understand now what people go on about . . . Well, it was better than the last time anyway, which is a big improvement.

Luke had found me, as I hoped he would. I didna really want to walk back through the forest on ma own an' I wanted him to come an' say sorry so I could say sorry an' we could sort it out. I was really embarrassed about arguing over nothing an' his dad knowing what it was about, it was all so awkward, but not now.

He picked me up – well, pulled me to ma feet really as Luke is no' that strong, still a wee bit skinny an' gangly. Anyway, he wrapped his arms around me, kissed me, looked deeply into ma eyes an' burped. Now I was no' expecting the burping part but he had just run through the woods an' had wind there, so I forgave him an' kissed his mortified face, red with shame, took his hand an' walked home with him.

When we got in there was a note from his dad an' Claire, to say they'd gone out for the evening. It was only seven o' clock. We looked at each other an' we didn't need to say anything. I knew what his face meant, what his eyes meant. I was bloody terrified, as I followed him up the stairs into the flowery bedroom. But I wanted this too – it was the only thing that would make it all right again an' it had been me who was the problem an' I couldn't see how I could hold out much longer. It was stupid anyway, he loved me, I loved him, and alone in the house what else could I expect?

We lay down shakily on the big 'adult' double bed,

64

cuddled an' talked for a wee while, then he pushed me gently away from him an' looked at me for a while, which was kinda nice an' gave me time to remember to breathe in an' out, important really if things were to go any further.

We reached the usual HALT! stage in record time. This is where I normally have a panic attack an' decide getting Luke as far away from me as possible is my only chance of survival, except this time I didna push his hand away or wait for him to sigh, tut an' pull his clothes back on again, in fact I helped him take them off. I couldna believe what I was doing. I removed one of his socks! I was so proud of maself! The sock territory is one I had never ventured into before. I was pleased with ma progress – we even laughed.

Previously in this type of situation we never laughed. I always took the whole thing so seriously I often forgot to smile even. But we were laughing an' smiling an' kissing an' talking quietly. I didna think it was supposed to be this much fun and kinda nice an' tender.

Suddenly we were naked. I am sure it wasn't sudden at all but it was a shock to the system to look down in the daylight at both of us naked. We had not seen each other fully naked before – normally we were thankfully covered by some form of clothing or some-one's coat, or some parent's duvet at a house party they knew nothing about. But now this was the real thing an' it was OK, he couldn't see ma birthmark on ma bum an' he thought I couldn't see that he still had chickenpox scars. Somehow it didn't matter that this was really embarrassing an' awkward 'cos we were smiling. It was good, even exciting, which it hadna been before – before it had been scary, frightening, nervy an' made ma stomach taught with fear. Now ma stomach was flipping over for all the right reasons.

We began slowly an' there were a few near misses which hurt as Luke misaimed an' bashed himself into ma leg but it was OK an' made me laugh.

Then he did it. His willy was inside me an' although it hurt a wee bit at first as it went in, it was-n't agony, it didna make me scream in pain, it did fit, an' it wasna too big – I think he was disappointed about that bit. He'd told me the condom would be too small for him as he was trying to put it on earlier, until I explained to him it was inside out! I don't even know how I knew that – probably one of the science lessons I wasna chucked out of. My God, if Miss Hall could see how we were following her instructions she would be livid. I think that although they taught us how to put a condom on at school they firmly believed that we would never need to use one if we were good girls and boys.

I couldna believe at first that this was it an' we were doing it an' it was all OK and we'd done it right an' were both alive an' well, no vital organs injured, no parents walking in an' being greeted with Luke's bum. It was a success an' I enjoyed it. I didna scream an' throw maself around the bed writhing in ecstasy but I liked it, ma tummy definitely flipped over an' I want to take it up as a new hobby, with Luke, occasionally.

LUKE

'I love you.'

I know she does, she keeps telling me every five minutes! But it's good, it's sincere, which it wasn't before. Before it was unsteady.

It's been really good the last couple of days, being together – we haven't argued once. I know it's not just the sex but that's a big part of it. It was the final thing we had to sort out. I am so glad we did. I can't believe I have gone this long without it. It's like the best thing ever, after *Star Wars* and the great George Lucas obviously.

We are a real couple. I'm sure people look at me differently, like they must know what we get up to, and think what a lucky sod I am. The whole condom thing is still well embarrassing though – there's no getting around that. They are just so weird. They smell funny and are awkward to put on and so inconvenient. Not that I am some master of love now, but I have had the need to use them a few times over the last three days I am proud to say, though unfortunately that means we have used up the supply carefully provided by my brother. Which leads us down to the chemist this morning. Now the decision . . .

'You go in. You're the bloke.'

Isla's weak suggestion fails to impress or sway me. No way am I going in there to buy those things.

'No, you, you're the woman, and you don't get embarrassed about this stuff, you buy Tampax! That's pretty much the same, isn't it?' A good case, well-made, honest, and factual in parts, I like to think.

'We'll toss a coin then. Heads it's you, tails it's me.' She takes the upper hand with a flick of the coin and it lands decidedly heads up. Not good. She gives me the LOOK! I cave in. Marching into the chemist without a care in the world is harder than it looks, as I sneak past the Blue Rinse Brigade at the prescriptions counter with their purchases firmly clasped to their huge scary bosoms. How come young women have breasts and older women have bosoms? Maybe something happens when you hit seventy and your boobs begin to defy gravity and have to have a name change. Anyway, I digress. I must make a purchase, but which condoms to choose?

A colourful array lies before me, next to a selection

of pregnancy tests! Why would you put these next to the condoms? It's a bit late for condoms if you are reaching for the extortionately priced 'Predictor Kits', isn't it? Well, better safe than sorry, I had to choose. Mates or Durex? Extra Safe or Ribbed? Flavoured or Glow in the Dark? Totally confusing. I think I'll play it safe seeing as we are novices in this game, plus I don't want the woman at the till to think I am a perve.

'Hello. Thank you. Yes. Uummm, cheers. Just these please. OK?' I babble everything in the wrong order and stand nervously waiting while the shop assistant takes what seems an inordinate amount of time to put my money in the till and give me the change. I almost tell her to keep it, except it's a tenner.

'Would you like a bag?'

Of course I want a bag, I want them in the bag, and preferably not a see-through one. Why do I feel like I am committing a crime? In fact, I am a saviour! Keeping the population down, costing the government less money, preventing Mr and Mrs Kelman from having heart attacks and generally being a respectable citizen. I should be awarded, knighted and given the condoms for free!

I escape with my purchase shoved under my arm and make for the exit. Isla is grinning widely, no doubt at my reddening face and increasingly rapid walk, which breaks into a run as I escape the glare of the Blue Rinse Brigade, heaving bosoms and double chins wobbling with disapproval as I sprint past them. How do they know? Do they have Ribbed condom radar?

Once we get near home we finally stop feeling so guilty about buying the product of sin. As we walk up the path we hope that Dad and Claire are out as normal. It's a bit strange, in some ways, because although me and Isla are sorted out now, the problem has been removed and we can move on, Dad and Claire are still around. I feel sort of adult-like and I can't stop grinning, but then they almost get in the way because they treat us like another couple, which we are not ready for – at least I am not.

The thing that bothers me is that Dad and Claire don't seem to care what we do, where we go, when we come in, or anything really, as long as we are out of their way. I thought my dad might interfere a bit more, or lay down the law, or at least grace me with the famous 'While you are under my roof you will do as I say' speech. I am almost disappointed that we haven't been treated to that. I'm sure my mum would have gone to the effort. I know I shouldn't complain

71

and should embrace this new-found freedom to do whatever I want, but somehow it's too much and it's a bit scary. Dad keeps trying to talk to me about Isla and me and is not quite getting it right. He has been removed from my life for so long that he doesn't really have much of a place in it any more. I've moved on and got on and he has been left behind, back when I was eight. He doesn't really know how to talk to me or what to say 'cos he's always going to be in the wrong. I definitely do not want to talk to him about me or anything to do with me and he keeps trying to include me in his new life, which I can never have a real part in.

As we approach the back door we can hear them in the kitchen, with their Mozart blasting out of the CD player. As we walk in they greet us.

'Hello, you two. Had a nice walk into town then? What are you doing today? We were thinking of going to Fistral beach to have a go at bodyboarding. Want to join us?'

Grrrr . . . Claire's fake 'I'm such a lovely stepmother' show is really getting annoying. She asks so many questions that she doesn't leave you any time to answer before she's on to the next! The Spanish Inquisition could have learned a lot from her.

'No thanks. We've already made plans to go surfing on our own.' I get my answer in quickly while Claire comes up for air. Now I am totally aware this sounds spoilt but I don't want to go surfing with them. I had it all planned in my head, just me and Isla on our own. I want to teach her what I know, show her Fistral beach myself. I don't want to have to listen to Claire discuss politics and the state of the government with my dad all day while he constantly tries to get Claire and me to bond. I am surprised by the Queen of Calm's reaction though as my dad gets ready to intervene. She actually stops him. Normally she loves him sticking up for her.

'Oh, for God's sake, Tom, don't bother. It's clear he doesn't want anything to do with me,' and she storms out of the kitchen, brushing newspapers and the breakfast crumbs on to the floor as she sweeps out of the room.

'Luke, a walk, now.' This from my dad. I have pushed it too far, but I wasn't being rude, I really do want to spend the day with Isla. Everything is so good with us at the moment. My dad walks slowly down the path at the side of the house and I presume I am to follow him. He doesn't turn round to look at me. This means trouble. When we were little my dad never shouted at us, he would just say in a quiet, calm voice exactly what he expected of us and you sort of did it 'cos the calm voice was scarier than my mum shouting in her high-pitched one.

He sits down on the nearest bench on the edge of the woods and waits for me. I stand, as I don't know what else to do. He gestures for me to sit down, so I do, reluctantly, like I am giving in to him in some way.

'Why do you dislike her so much?' The question is so honest it shocks me. I feel I can't lie.

'I don't know. 'Cos she took you away from us? It's all her fault.' I don't really know why she annoys me so much. If she was just some woman at school, or college, or someone my mum knew, I probably would never have noticed her, or would have at least been polite, but because of who she is and what she has done I feel this way.

'It wasn't just Claire, you know. It was me, your mum – we weren't in love any more. We were friends, companions, but nothing more. Claire was someone who I was interested in, we had more in common than your mum and I. We were attracted to each other and there was nothing I could do. I was miserable, Luke, really unhappy with my life, and she came along and changed all that.' He is explaining it to me and I can hear him, but I don't want to know this.

'Look, it's nothing to do with me, you and Mum. Just don't expect me to like her, OK.' I think this is fair enough but he gets me with the next question.

'Why not?'

I can't think of a reasonable answer so I think I'll give shouting a go. 'Because she is not my mum! You left us on our own. Mum is lonely and I am a mess and Matthew hasn't got a dad and you wouldn't pay our maintenance and you are so wrapped up in her you don't even care about me and Isla and what I am doing. You are not even a proper dad!' There is no particular order or arrangement to my words, they just jump out of my mouth and fall all over the path.

'Luke, I understand you are angry and confused and I know I haven't handled things well, but I am trying now. You just need to give me a chance, to let me in. It's not that I don't care – you won't let me care. You won't let me talk to you or ask you questions. How can I be your dad if you won't let me?'

This is too much. He is so calm and controlled and has all his thoughts neatly filed in order and I don't. I have to get away.

ISLA

When he got back, Luke's dad was shaking and looked really mad. I wondered what had happened an' where Luke was. I didna know what to say. I hardly knew the man. Claire had gone into town to have a change of scene so it was just me and him if Luke were no' coming back for a bit. I felt really awkward like I'd caused the argument, which I knew I hadna, but still I felt a wee bit to blame for the way Luke had acted.

Tom sat down at the table, crumpled up in a chair. He didn't speak an' I couldna stand the silence. I didna know him well enough for a silence to be comfortable.

'Are you all right?' A stupid question I know, but I had nothing else.

'Hmmmm. No. Tell me, Isla, does Luke talk to you about all this? This mess?' He was wandering around the room, half making a cup of tea, half looking at the door hoping for Luke to appear. I knew he was talking about the divorce, at least I presumed that was the mess he was talking about.

'Not really. He's mentioned it a few times, like when there was the problem with the money an—' There I stopped maself. Who was I to comment on money an' divorce an' their family life?

'No, go on, I know what you are going to say. The money. It was really awkward for us that month. We had a lot of money going out and we were in a difficult position. I missed one or two payments and the money stopped for Matt because he turned eighteen.'

I wished he hadna explained. I was so embarrassed, squirming in ma chair. This conversation was not for me, this was for Luke but he wasna around to hear it, having stormed off somewhere probably, having my brooding walk along the cliff tops, the tortured hero. But it looked like I was the only one Tom could talk to or had to talk to at that moment.

I made a suggestion. 'Shall we go for a drive?' Brave, as I still had no idea what to say, but a walk could be dangerous as we might run into Luke an' I wasna sure if they were ready for each other yet. Luckily Tom agreed, went an' got his camera an' car keys an' off we set for the coast, away from Newquay, away from Luke an' Claire.

We drove for half an hour or so up the coast to a place called Padstow. Apparently, according to Tom, there is a famous chef who lives there, called Rick Stein, I think. We didna meet him but we did see his restaurant an' I took a photo of it with my camera to show ma dad. After we'd had a pasty each we decided to go for a walk around the town, which was really sweet, with whitewashed cottages an' a pretty harbour – the stereotypical Cornish town, except it was more than that.

We moved up on to the hills an' found the coastal path and walked in silence for a wee while. It was OK by then, the silence thing. I've never been good with silences, particularly with people I don't know, but it seemed to be what Tom wanted. Then we stopped an' sat down so he could change his lens. His hobby was photography. He was really good at it, I'd seen quite a few of his photos before. He started explaining the difference between the lens and the exposure he need-ed for a shot of the sea from this distance. I didna understand a lot of it, but it was interesting an' some of it made sense. I was settling into familiarity when he pulled the rug out from under ma feet.

'What's Luke like? Tell me about him.'

What did he mean? This was his dad speaking, he

knows what Luke's like. I didna answer so he carried on.

'What I mean is, tell me about Luke – his personality, why you are with him. I feel like I hardly know him.'

Now I understood. He wanted me to fill in the gaps, the bits he's missed or the parts Luke wouldn't tell him. It was funny the way Luke's dad treated us like adults, but I sort of liked it. It was very different to my mum and dad.

So I told him about Luke – what he was like at school, how we'd met, how kind he was to me when I first started school. About the job we'd had at 'Dave's Belly', and about the day I walked out an' took money from the till. About the next thing, when I came home to find that ma sister had been killed, nine years old, run over, or hit by a car, whatever you want to call it. I told him shakily about Luke and how he helped me, looked after me, brought me slowly back into the world. How I couldn't cry, how guilty I felt having been horrible to Hannah for years an' then she was gone an' I'd had my chance an' missed it. I think that how's Tom felt about Luke a little bit.

'It's like I've missed Luke growing up and missed out on being his dad and now he won't let me back in and it's too late.'

Except it wasn't too late for them. Nothing was wrong with Luke an' his dad. They were both well, both adults (sort of) able to communicate, able to sort this out. It wasna a real big mess, I told Tom, it just needed some time, talking an' patience on both sides.

'It's easy for you to say that. You've nothing to be angry with your parents about. I have a new partner to consider, a new family to try to balance out with the old one and their needs too. I know, I know, it's not as simple as that and I can't even begin to imagine what you went through with your sister and what you still must be feeling, and I know I have the chance to put this right and try and build a relationship with Luke. I know . . . '

He seemed to have run out of breath an' energy an' talking and so had I. I looked at ma watch an' it was already well into the afternoon. We'd been there for three hours. I wondered where Luke was an' if he were OK. He must be so confused about the whole thing. He knows he's being a pain in the arse with Claire but he's still mad with his dad and he takes it out on her. I had explained this to Tom earlier, not that he didna already know it. It's just that he didn't know what to do about it.

LUKE

Great holiday. So far I've run off twice and sat on this beach throwing stones into the water. If I'm not careful the tourist board will start charging people to come and look at the mad old beach man who glowers and mutters under his breath and can't skim a stone to save his life. Some life.

I am a mess and I don't even know why. My mum is fine really, she is probably happier without Dad, and Dad is very happy in some weird sad way with Claire, and no matter how much she loves her contact lenses and how boring she is she does love my dad. Isla loves me and I think I am pretty much in love with her if that's what we are calling it, so what the bloody hell is my problem? I just don't like my dad with another woman who is trying to be part of my life. She isn't my mum and I refuse to ever accept her as my stepmum, but I am going to have to accept her as my dad's wife. They've been married for two years now, I think.

ARGGHHH! I am even annoying myself with all this crap. What do I care? Let him get on with his life and do what he wants, he always did. I need to grow up and not worry so much about everyone else and get on with my own life. There's no point in taking it out on Claire. It could have been anyone who came along and seduced my dad and stole him away from his loving wife and two children, ripping apart the family. Great. Good to see I am dealing with this in a mature and sensible way.

There is a group of people on the beach now, it's not so quiet at lunch time. They have all got surf boards which they are unloading from their VW camper vans. Cool wheels. It would be so good to have a car or a van and go off travelling whenever you wanted and not have to rely on anyone. I can't wait till I am seventeen. Mum has promised me driving lessons. I know how to drive anyway, Ripper let me have a go in his Mini a couple of times, just up the track to his house, not on the road or anything, and it was brilliant. I couldn't get used to the separate pedals to start with but I think after a few lessons I should pass my test. Mum and Matt both passed first time, I hope it runs in the family.

The surfers are heading out to the sea. The conditions don't look that good, the waves are quite flat today – not that I am a surfing expert. There's three lads and two girls. They've certainly got the right gear – wetsuits, boards and all that. Their boards look really battered. I wonder where they are from – they look really tanned and different. Definitely not from Maidstone. I wish I were brave enough to talk to them. I'm bored on my own, done enough thinking for one day. I want to have some fun now. If Isla were here we could wander over and watch them surf, but I'll look a twat on my own, a sad loser sat on the beach sulking. God, I've been a pain in the arse.

Maybe if I skulk around their van when they get out, they'll talk to me. They look older than me, more experienced – in what I don't know, but definitely more experienced. I wander over to the van and see that there is still someone in there. I jump with surprise, annoyingly.

'All righ', mate? Can I help ya?'

Australian. Sounds like someone off *Neighbours*. 'Ummm . . . nope, just having a look at the van. Sorry.' Why do I always apologise when I haven't actually done anything wrong?

'Sure, no worries. Surfer, are ya?'

Excellent! 'No. Well, not yet. I want to have a go.

Are you from Australia?' Stupid question, I can tell he is from the accent, the hair, the tan. Great. Now he'll think I am the Village Idiot.

'Yep, that's right, over here on a tour, mate. And yourself?'

OK, he's still talking to me. Try to relax, Luke. He is just a human being who is taking you seriously and has not told you to piss off yet.

'I'm from Maidstone . . . near London?' Why do we lie to tourists and resort to saying we live near London, as if it's the only place they could ever have heard of in the UK?

'Haven't been to London yet, not much surf there. Just been around the south coast so far. Great country you've got here, mate. Fancy a surf then? Not much out there today, probably a good time to learn. What d'ya say?'

This was what I'd hoped he might offer. We move on to names and stuff – he is called Sam. The others introduce themselves as we wade into the water – Erika, Marcus, Kally, Ben and Danny. They all look really nice and friendly and shout out advice about how to sit on the board and when to turn for the wave. They use all these technical terms which I do not get, but I don't care – my holiday has finally started.

ISLA

Luke got hold of me on ma mobile about sixish and told me where he was an' invited me down. I felt a bit awkward leaving his dad, but Claire had come back an' they seemed to be OK with one another an' probably needed to talk. I said I'd go an' sort Luke out an' maybe we could all go to the beach together tomorrow or meet up or something. I didna want to promise anything in case Luke said no.

Luke told me he had met some Australians down on the beach an' was staying there for a barbecue. I was a bit jealous at first 'cos I could hear laughter an' shouting in the background an' I knew I would be a wee bit shy around new people, but he sounded so happy I couldna say no, plus I wanted to see him. I'd missed him.

By the time I got to the edge of the forest he was there waiting for me with a huge smile. We kissed an' I quickly told him about ma day with his dad an he seemed so grateful. He seemed much better, lighter somehow. We ran down the beach an' reached the barbecue area quickly. There were a few people still playing on the beach, running in and out of the water, throwing a frisbee, an' a couple walking their dog, an' then there were Luke's friends.

I liked them instantly, which I never do normally. Ben an' Sam were tall, skinny an' very good looking, with messy blonde hair an' scruffy clothes. They were really funny an' told stories all night, taking the piss out of each other the whole time. They were from Queensland in Australia. Then there was Danny and Kally – I think they were together, a couple. They were from America – Portland I think they said, not that the name meant much to me, an' then there was Erika an' Marcus who were from Sweden. They were definitely a couple an' had met up with the others in France.

Luke had spent most of the afternoon in the water, judging from his prune-like hands. He said they'd been teaching him how to surf an' that he had not got very far but it was cool. They all talked all at once, over each other, shouting an' laughing, competing for centre stage.

I talked mostly to Erika – she was lovely, an' the quietest. She an' Marcus were making their way up through the UK, even as far as the Outer Hebrides! I've no' even been there maself. I was impressed. I told her about Edinburgh an' the best places to go an' she told me about their travels so far. I got the impression she wanted her and Marcus to be on their own again but was happy to spend a wee bit of time with the lively crowd they had met.

Marcus an' Luke set up a volleyball competition an' were sorted for the evening.

It was one of the most relaxed times I had on the holiday. Erika was telling me how to surf an' that she wasna very good either. She invited me down to Fistral the next morning. We'd have to get there at five-thirty so I could get in some time before the professional posers turned up, i.e. the lads, an' Kally, who was apparently very good.

When Luke ran over later an' flopped down on to the sand next to me, for a moment I was so pleased to be with him, to see him, that I forgot about everything that had happened that day. The others teased Luke an' me about how much Luke went on about me whilst they were teaching him to surf an' how miserable he looked when they first saw him. They didn't ask why, an' we were both glad.

They told us they were staying for another week an'

we were welcome to come along with them in one of the vans, tomorrow or any day. It was good to listen to their stories an' hear about the places they've travelled to. I felt a bit silly but I asked them how they could afford the travelling an' not having a proper job. And what were they going to do when they eventually had to go home?

They laughed at me an' I felt naive. Sam explained to me that they travel until they run out of money, then they stop for a bit an' get a job in a bar, on a farm, with the boats, whatever is around, save up a bit an' then move on. It sounded fantastic but I couldna see maself doing it. It seemed so reckless an' carefree an' almost too simple. I know ma parents would go mad if I said I was going to go off travelling for an indefinite amount of time. Ma dad would want a five-year plan an' details of what job I would come home to an' would no' be happy about me working ma way around countries an' sleeping in a van an' surfing all day long. It sounded like heaven to me right then. Maybe I could? Why not?

LUKE

We have had the best day today. We spent all of it at Fistral again, with Sam and everyone. I managed to stay upright for longer than ten seconds today! Isla was most impressed. She gave up after a couple of hours and sat on the beach with Erika, taking photos. Dad had lent her one of his cameras as hers is not that good. She's getting well into it and has gone through two films today – she says Dad is going to show her how to develop them later.

Things are so much better on that front. I actually spoke to Claire yesterday and had a whole civilised conversation with her this morning – as civilised as it gets at half-past six, anyway. We had to get up early for the surf and Claire happened to be up too. I thought I had better start behaving as it was looking like she had had enough of me and I don't want to cause trouble for my dad.

So I learned about the Break today – that's where the wave forms over the shore of the reef – and I learned how to do a Switchfoot, which is exactly what it sounds, spinning your feet round to face the other way. I didn't stay on long after this – a bit ambitious, but I think it could be heard on the beach that I am a natural. Apparently it's going to be 'flat as a board' tomorrow so Isla and I are off for a day on our own.

I love this surf thing – the language, the clothes, the people. They're all so friendly – apart from Kally, that is. She is serious out on the waves and doesn't join in with the talking and joking and finds me, the 'rookie dude', a 'pain in the butt'. Surfing's like a lifestyle – travelling and having no cares in the world other than what to eat for your next meal and what country to go and see next. I wish I could do this. I know probably everyone wishes they could stay on holiday for ever and never go home but for me it's not just Cornwall that's so great, it's these people too. They don't care about jobs or houses or mortgages or any of the things I presume I will have to worry about one day, just like my mum living on whatever is left over at the end of every month. It's just a capitalistic world and a system I don't want to become part of. Well, that's what Sam says and I agree with him. I have never talked about stuff like this before – it's not quite politics, it's more discussions about life. Not that I would ever admit to Claire that I had been having 'discussions', she'd be so smug.

Despite the fact that Sam is trying to turn me into a Marxist by lecturing me on all that is bad in our world, I have had a great day and am starting to get a tan and look almost as brown as the rest of them. I reckon I could fit in well here, apart from the fact that I am joining the RAF and still living with my mum and on holiday with my dad and haven't got a camper van, or blonde matted hair. Apart from that I am practically one of them, dude.

I need to make some changes. My life has been so ordinary so far. I want to get out there, explore, see the world. All I have seen is Maidstone and a bit of Florida which, according to Kally, isn't really America anyway as it's a tourist trap. I haven't gone anywhere or done anything other than go to school! I'm nearly seventeen and what have I done? If I died tomorrow I would have regrets that I hadn't had any adventures.

I tell Isla this and she instantly knows how I feel. I know it's not just because of spending the week with Sam and Danny but that is definitely what has got me thinking. I am so eager to get on with my life and stop whingeing about all the bad stuff that has happened and go places and do things – I don't know what things, but I want to be out there doing them, maybe even here in Cornwall. This is one of the best places I have ever been and Sam says it's just as good as Oz. Kally takes the piss when I get excited and say I am going to stay here.

'Yeah right. Uh huh. Your mom gonna let you stay down here and not go off to airplane school then?'

I don't know why she doesn't like me, but I don't care. Isla and I are going to talk about it later 'cos I can see the same thing in her eyes.

'Leave him alone, Kal, why shouldn't he stay here? It's a great place,' Sam interjects.

I like Sam. I would love to live his life. I know I can't really stay here but you don't want to be told that by some girl with badly bleached hair and over-tanned skin who is only a few years older than me anyway. *She's* not so perfect.

Later on when we are on our own, Isla and I talk. We are walking back to the house, wet, tired and tanned. Well, I am – Isla has just added to her extensive freckle collection, though if they joined up she would be more tanned than any of us.

'What are you thinking?'

This must be the most overused question girls ask. Why must they know what we are thinking at all times? It's as if they need to monitor our every thought, hoping that it's about them, in a positive light of course. Sometimes I risk answering 'Nothing' but even though this is often the truth girls never believe it. They seem to be incapable of having a similar thought pattern to men. Sometimes I really do think – well, nothing. You know, just random odd thoughts like 'beans, running, white paint, beer, tired, breasts, maths homework, blonde hair . . . ' Nothing that would make any sense if you tried to explain it so you just say 'Nothing' and then get in real trouble. So it's easier to answer and, well, lie.

'Um, I was thinking about you?' I test this one out. We appear to have a winner! Isla is smiling, almost a self-satisfied grin which says 'Mmmhmm, yes, I thought you might be thinking about me, as so you should be, young man'. Now she is waiting for the rest. I need more.

'I was thinking about you and, uuuum . . . staying here in Cornwall for ever or going off with Ben and Sam and everyone and travelling for a bit. What do you think?' Give the girl a chance to speak herself, I don't want to hog the whole conversation now, do I? I can tell by looking at her face she has already thought about this. But I have a feeling she is going to be sensible. Her lips are too straight, she is not looking dreamy enough. I have just offered her a dream lifestyle and she looks like she is contemplating forty years inside!

'Well, it would be lovely, but you know we canna. You've got your RAF and we've got college and your mum is on her own. We've got a few days left, why don't we just chill and enjoy them and worry about the boring stuff when we get home?'

A sensible proposition I know, but I don't want to be sensible any more. Time for a change.

ISLA

I'd always thought Luke was a bit of a dreamer at school but I guessed he'd grow out of it when he got older. I think I might have been wrong. When we sat down for breakfast on the last day of the holiday he announced to his dad an' Claire the decision he had made the night before. I had a fair idea what he was going to say as he'd kept me awake all night talking about it, asking me over an' over 'What do you think?', 'Is that a good idea?', 'That sounds OK, doesn't it?' Apart from smothering him with ma pillow an' telling him to go back to his own room there wasn't much I could do to shut him up.

It was weird – after sorting out the whole sex thing we'd decided to have our own rooms anyway, an' to sneak in an' out of one another's rooms in the night. It made it seem less of an issue, an' less serious if we did that. I wasna ready to share a room with Luke like a married couple or something. Still, it was nice falling asleep with each other afterwards. We'd had sex quite a few times by this point and I was beginning to feel like I was in a proper relationship, nearly like an adult. Luke however was still acting like a dreamy kid.

'The jam is running out no point getting some more later is there oh and I am not joining the RAF any more because I don't need any qualifications to teach surfing and diving. Is there any more toast, Dad?'

I choked on ma slice of toast an' it sounded like Claire was struggling too. Tom just calmly passed Luke another slice of toast and looked thoughtful for a wee while, whilst we all fell silent, Luke no' looking quite so calm an' in control now. He was ready an' armed for an argument an' had all his facts ready for battle.

'When did you reach this decision then, Luke?' Tom was so impressive, so calm, so thoughtful and clever in his questions. He didna shout or even raise his voice, he didn't immediately say 'No you are bloody well not' or slam out of the room in a temper. Maybe I'd been around ma dad for too long. Obviously there were men in the world who could ask questions before shouting the odds. Luke went in for the kill.

'Ages ago. I don't want to just become part of the system, a small cog turning in a big wheel, making money for a greedy government who will take most of my money and hand me back a tiny sum so that I can have my bins collected once a week. It's a terrible state, Dad, the world – just one big capitalist society.' Luke sighed dramatically at the end of his performance and I could have sworn I saw Claire smother a smile as she raised her coffee cup to her lips. Luke's dad sighed and took a sip of tea before making his next comment.

'Luke, if you don't want to join the RAF any more, that's fine. It's obviously your decision, but choose your own reasons why – don't be swayed by what other people tell you about the world. Go out and make your own mind up. I hated my job for years when I first started out in the business but I stuck it out and now I quite like it. If you don't think you can stick it out, then change now, but do it for the right reasons. People come and go and leave behind their opinions, often wanting you to agree with them so they can justify their own choices. You must make your own choices, Luke.'

Wow! I think I got what he was saying. Luke was looking a bit annoyed so he must have got it too.

Later on when Tom an' Claire had gone for a final walk Luke and I talked.

'I want to travel and it's not just 'cos I met Sam and everyone, though I know that has helped me decide. But my dad's right, annoying as it is to say that. I do need to make my own choices. I'm going to change my AS options, to media studies, no more maths for me, and I am going to think about what I really want to do. I want to stay at college but after that I don't know, but it won't be living in Maidstone, that's for sure. There's too much else to do, too many other places to go. It's so exciting, Isla!'

An' to him it was. All I wanted was to keep things as they were. If Luke was going to go off and travel or whatever, where would that leave me? After these last two weeks I had realised how much he meant to me. It's not just some teenage crush as ma dad seems to think. We've got closer on this holiday, more than we were before, an' to think that that might not last an' might change an' that he might leave an' go to Australia or America or wherever is a scary thought. I suddenly didn't know where I was any more.

LUKE

Mum has been so glad to see me home that I still can't tell her. I know I should. I mean I've been back for a week and had plenty of opportunity; college started yesterday and she's been back at school teaching for a week now so I have to get on with it. I don't know why I think she will care so much or be hurt – it's not as if the RAF is the only option or career choice she would approve of, but somehow I know she won't react well. She is managing not to ask me too many questions about the holiday or Claire so I just tell her little bits. I don't feel quite as badly about Claire as I used to but I feel I sort of have to keep on hating her for my mum. I don't want her to think I like Claire or that she could be a mother figure to me.

I've done as much telly-watching as I can be arsed to do, so I go downstairs to survey the contents of the fridge. It's a dark day when you find the fridge empty. Normally when I have been at school or work and I come home the fridge is a mirage, an oasis of calm amidst the books, washing and paraphernalia I bring home with me. This time though, despite being full of food, it doesn't offer any comfort. I realise with horror and surprise that I am Not Hungry! I am a teenager, a growing lad, I should be consuming vast quantities of food in order to cope with the growth spurts that keep attacking but I. AM. NOT. HUNGRY. I am not hungry, not even mildly peckish, I don't think I could even handle a snack. The shock almost causes my legs to buckle. This is bad. This is a serious situation. Not since the day we got our GCSE results have I felt so weak and confused and depleted of all my energy stores. I can stand the guilt no longer. I have to tell her.

If she comes into the kitchen before I make it to the back door for a smooth, sharp exit then it's . . . Before I can even finish my thought I realise the Gods must hate me because Mum breezes in. Poor innocent, loving Mum, who sacrificed everything for me, went through eighteen hours of agonising labour to bring me into this world, putting her whole career on hold to bring me up, pinning up every crap painting I brought home on the fridge, even wearing the perfume I made her from crushed rose petals which smelt of wee, and this is how I repay her? A traitorous son am I. Crippled by the guilt I collapse into the nearest available chair and confess my sins.

'Mum, I have something to tell you.'

Dramatic pause as I wait for her to sit down.

'I am not going into the RAF'. I squeeze my eyes shut as I utter the words that will seal my fate as outcast son. I tentatively open them and look up, expecting to see the fury in her face. She looks OK. What's going on here? Maybe she hasn't heard me. I take a deep breath and try again, repeating myself . . . still no smoke coming out of her ears.

'Mum? Did you hear me?'

She nods. This is worse than I thought it'd be. I have rendered her silent, mute, immobilised with anger. She can't bear to speak to me. The silence is agony.

'Well???' Anything is better than the silence.

'OK, love, if you really don't want to. It seems such a shame though. You used to love going to Cadets. It seems a shame to waste it, but then I suppose you do grow out of the things you used to like, as you get older. Your tastes change and you want different things. Do you want some tea?'

Tea? TEA?? Do I want some tea? Has the woman gone mad? This is my future we are talking about here. Why isn't she screaming and shouting and begging me to reconsider? Why isn't she asking me what my plans are now? How am I going to live? How will I survive? That kind of thing.

'Mum? You're not annoyed then? Don't you want to know what my plans are?' I can't believe I am having to feed her the parent lines. I'll be handing her the manual 'How to be an interfering parent' soon. I thought she'd written the book!

'Only if you want to tell me, love. Why would I be annoyed? It's your life. I wouldn't want you to do something you didn't want to, would I? Silly!' And with this she ruffles my hair, plants a kiss on the top of my head and begins cooking, humming to herself as she does so.

Now this is unprecedented. Normally we would have to draw up a 'gameplan' of the future or at the very least make a long list to try and organise my life in some way. What has happened to the interfering mother I used to know and be annoyed by? Time for drastic measures. I will have to contact the Guru, that is, my brother.

'Hello, can I speak to Matthew Field please?'

I hate the polite telephone voice I put on, it just doesn't seem to be controllable. I suddenly start speaking like I have gone to private school all my life and have my own personal elocution teacher. It's particularly embarrassing when you ring up somewhere like a university hall of residence. That's where Matthew is. It's basically a big building with lots of tiny cell-like rooms in it, divided into floors. There's eight students to a block, four blocks on a floor, three floors, that's 96 students per building. So somewhere amongst the 96 lurks my brother and someone has to find him for me, despite my sounding like I have three plums in my mouth and know Prince Charles and the Queen intimately.

'What (belch) floor's he on?'

Important information which has conveniently gone out of my head, slightly aided by the burping down the phone. Mum comes to the rescue.

'Room 19, third floor.'

I can hear the gut-wrenching sigh of the person on the other end of the phone, probably contemplating whether they can be bothered to run up three flights of stairs or just put the phone down on me, which has happened before. I hear him running off – this sounds good. About five minutes later I hear footsteps come pounding down the stairs and Matthew, shouting 'Hang on, I'm coming!' – as if I am going to put the phone down after waiting for five minutes – as Mum leaves the room with a meaningful look, pointing subtly at her watch.

'Hello?'

'All right Matt? It's me.'

'All right. Umm . . . how are you?' It's strange, when we are at home together we talk bollocks for ages, rambling on about all kinds of rubbish, yet put us on the phone to one another and we have nothing to say.

'Yeah, fine. You?'

'Yeah, all right thanks.' Scintillating discussion. How we've progressed from monosyllabic teenagers. I decide to cut to the chase.

'Look, Matt, major situation going on here. I got back from Newquay today and—' Before I can get to the heart of the matter, Matt decides he wants a chat now.

'Newquay! How was it? We had such a mad summer there two years ago, Ripper and I camped down there. Did you get to Fistral Bay and The Newquay Arms? Definitely one of the best pubs there.'

I have to stop this before he goes off on one about the good old days before he was a serious student. Serious my arse.

'Shut up, Matt! Look, Mum is being weird.' I stop for him to pay attention and take in what I am saying, before I carry on. 'I told her I am not joining the RAF any more and—'

'WHAT???' Interrupted again. 'You are joking? Why not? What the hell's happened?'

After practically deafening me Matt lets me get a word in. 'I'm just not, OK? It's not important, but Mum is being weird, she's not freaking out, unlike you, she's just saying "OK, love, whatever you want love," whilst humming and stuff. And the worst bit is she's wearing make-up and she's done something weird to her hair.'

I await a sensible reply.

I don't get one.

'Maybe the aliens landed while you were in Newquay and replaced her with a Stepford Mom.'

'Be serious, Matt. She's gone funny.' I can't find any decent words to describe my mum with.

'Grow up, Luke. Look, she's probably just met someone.'

WHAT??

'What do you mean? Who?'

WHO??

'I dunno. Some bloke or something. Maybe that's

why she's chilled, 'cos she's happy?' Matthew sounds annoyingly smug and superior about his deduction and it does make more sense than the alien theory. But a man? My mum? We finish up the conversation with the usual.

'You'll have to come and stay, mate, when I get a house, yeah?'

Yeah right!

'Yeah, sure, Matt. See ya.'

Maybe she has met someone, but who, and when? I have to find out.

ISLA

Luke's confessional seemed to go so well I was jealous. Not only was his dad cool an' calm but his mum didna seem to throw a fit either. He seemed to have forgotten the whole RAF thing though as his curiosity was now taken up with his mum. Matthew had planted the ridiculous idea into Luke's head that his mum was seeing someone an' Luke had made it his mission to discover the mystery man. He couldn't simply ask his mum about it so he was playing detective an' watching her every move to see if he could find out what she was up to.

I could not imagine his mum going out with anyone and neither could he.

'No, but do you think she is though?' For the third time on the phone that night he was asking the same question whilst I was trying to watch *EastEnders*. Serious stuff was going down in Albert Square an' I needed to pay attention.

'Luke, I don't know. We've been over this a

hundred times. So what if she is?' I know he couldna cope with it, poor lad. I think he might have had an Oedipal complex if it weren't for the fact that he doesn't know what one is.

'Isla, why don't *you* ask her? She likes you and you're a girl.'

There was no getting anything past this sharp cookie, was there?

'N.O. spells NO! Now bugger off an' let me do ma homework!'

I couldna admit to watching such trash an' the homework excuse seemed more plausible, especially as I knew he had loads to do himself. We seemed to have gone from very little at school to a terrifying amount at college. I wish someone had warned me then I might have . . . I don't know, I was going to say paid more attention at school, but then that's a load of rubbish. It's still too much work for Year 12, and too big a jump from being nagged by teachers in Year 11 to Year 12 where if you don't do your homework they don't say anything, they just tell you how many marks you've lost this module . . . shit, Luke was still talking in ma ear. I had to put the phone down, I had matters of ma own to deal with, after *EastEnders* obviously.

Luke had been trying to rope me into becoming

Watson to his Sherlock Holmes but I had ma own parents to deal with and they were a handful enough without taking on Luke's mum as well. I never realised having parents would turn out to be so difficult, such a responsibility, you can never truly relax an' forget about them, can you? Always worrying about what they will do next.

Take ma mum an' dad (take them, please?) for example. I had only been back from holiday for two weeks before they were up to their old tricks, namely interfering in ma life, again. I thought I would follow Luke's lead an' explain calmly an' in an adult way that I no longer wanted to be a nurse. No' some huge disaster, or crisis-inducing event, just the small matter that I now wanted to be a photographer. However if you are ma father apparently this is the end of the world, the end of his and ma life, an' it is at the very least a national disaster. If there had been a helpline for children having to deal with troublesome parents I would have been calling it that night. As it was, I had to deal with them all by maself.

'Dad, will you calm down, please? Look, I have tried the courses out for three whole weeks now. I don't like them, they are too hard, the teachers are crap and the courses are full of geeks. I want to be a photographer. At least I know what I want to do with my life now.' I thought this sounded reasonable, almost like I had a plan. But I knew what he would say next – *Where has this photography thing come from all of a sudden?*

'So where has this little photographing thing come from then? Hmm . . . overnight you decide to be a photographer when up till now you've wanted to be a nurse. No doubt tomorrow you'll want to be a zoo keeper, eh?'

A regular stand-up comedian ma dad, though being a zoo keeper would be interesting . . . I wonder what AS levels you need for that . . . but back to the matter in hand.

'Dad, it's not the end of the world. I am still doing English lit and biology, I am just swopping chem and physics for photography and theatre studies, that's all.' Reasonable, surely? Apparently not.

'That's all? That's all? You are only after changing your whole future! All that hard work an' for what? Nothing! So you can take some photos. It's not a proper career, Isla. Do you not think it might be a bit more difficult than that? You have changed since you got back from your holiday. It's that Luke, isn't it? He's put you up to this. I always said he was a bad influence on her, didn't I, Liz? I don't think she should see him any more if he's practically encouraging her to drop out. Liz?'

Now he was getting really red in the face an' pacing around the room a bit an' appealing to ma mum to support his team. I shouldha calmed him down at this point rather than joining him in the redness of the face competition but I was a wee bit annoyed too. How dare he tell me what to do an' who I can see! Who does he think he is?

'Luke had nothing to do with this! Do you no' think I can make up ma own mind then? He is no' a bad influence on me, in fact he's a very good one. If it hadna been for him I wouldna have ma maths GCSE! I will not stop seeing him just because you have always hated him. You are just using this as an excuse because you don't like him for whatever pathetic reason!'

Ma feminist rant and ma arsey tone of voice didna seem to convince him, so when all else fails appeal to the mother, the calming influence. 'Mum, what do you think? It's OK to change ma options at this stage, isn't it?' Now I knew I could depend on ma mum to at least pretend to consider ma sensible decision.

'Whatever you want, Isla. Hmm. It's your life.'

Now this I was not expecting. These were practically the very words Luke's mum had said to him, but when ma mum said them as she walked out of the room, in her quiet, flat, worn-out voice, they didna sound anywhere near the same.

LUKE

I've wanted to see the new *Lord of the Rings* film for ages and have read the book three times so when Mum suggested it for tonight I was well up for it. I knew the cast list, a very impressive one too, off by heart. The new multiplex beckoned as did the large tub of popcorn. I haven't been to the cinema with my mum for ages, not since *Bambi* or something embarrassing like that, but she was really keen to see the film. Isla was having a talk with her dad, so I decided to treat my mum to my delectable company for the evening.

I am glad we prebooked, admittedly with her credit card, but I am going to treat her to popcorn. The queue is massive. Never will I go to an opening night again, not unless protected with cricket pads for safety. My God, some people have no respect. I have just been battered by three women rushing to join the queue which is snaking its way out of the building and into the car park. Pensioners can be surprisingly strong, especially the ones with their little wheely trolleys. You'd never know they had it in them, would you? They look so innocent with their permed hair and pockets full of humbugs, the ruffians.

Mum and I find seats fairly near the front as she's forgotten her glasses, ignoring the numbers our tickets give us. Surely no one checks what seat you are in any more. We settle down, get comfy, arrange our coats on the seats next to us, hoping that no one will sit there. Cinemas always turn me into a sadist who loathes the human race. I always get a group of teenage girls sitting next to me who text each other incessantly throughout the film, giggling and chewing gum noisily, or a young couple with a baby who couldn't find a baby sitter that night so they bring the howling child with them and all the gear a baby needs which they proceed to place all over the seat and under your feet, muttering 'Sorry, sorry' in a loud stage whisper. If you are that sorry you should have stayed at home. So tolerant am I.

Mum nudges me out of my musings and signals that the film is about to start. I settle back and enjoy not only the amazing story, scenery and style of the film but also the delightful Cate Blanchett, who is such a stunner and of course a very talented actor too.

It's actor these days, isn't it, rather than actress, obviously more P.C. Hah! P.C., who wants to be P.C. anyway? You can't say anything these days without someone telling you it's Politically Incorrect. Whatever happened to freedom of speech?

As we leave the cinema Mum decides rather predictably that she needs the loo, so I wait for her on the other side of the foyer to avoid the mad rush of women around the Ladies. It's always the same huge queue for the women. No queue for the men, we must have larger bladders. Apparently there are only ever three or four cubicles in the Ladies, though you'd think they'd build more or offer them the use of the Men's which is nearly always empty, except in a pub, but even then it's a quick in and out job. I think women spend longer in the loo putting the world to rights, slagging off men, applying more lipstick and gossiping, whereas men use the bogs for their true purpose, pissing in. You'd never catch blokes chatting as they pee. Women are weird.

My mum comes out and is starting to make her way over to me, pushing through everyone, when a bloke takes her arm and stops her. Her face lights up and she gives him a kiss on the cheek. WHO is that? He has his back to me so I can't see his face. She chats to him for what seems like ages, then nods her head, laughs and points to me. He turns round and it's MR BLOODY CHAPMAN! No way! My science teacher – my *old* science teacher I hasten to add, so I wouldn't have thought he'd remember my mum from only one or two parents' evenings, so why are they talking and why on earth did she kiss him? They're saying good-bye, he nods to me, I nod back. What is going on? Mum comes over.

'Mum? Why did you . . . how do you know . . . ?'

Once again the teenage boy is rendered speechless by the behaviour of women. Mum understands my confusion and helps me out by saying, 'It's Mr Chapman, Luke. You remember him?'

Oh, how helpful.

'Of course I bloody do. I had to look at his face and try to decipher his spidery handwriting for two years, I know who he is!' What I really want to know is what is she doing acting like he is her friend, or worse?

'Mr Chapman and I met at a teachers' conference over the summer. We are in the same union and we got chatting.'

OK, that sounds OK. I am relieved. Not that I would mind if Mum had a boyfriend, just not my old science teacher. Obviously there is a line you do not cross and going out with your son's teacher is clearly crossing that line, but my mum knows that. We drive home to my mum humming a Beatles tune, *Love, love me do*. I tell myself it's a coincidence.

ISLA

Well, the gossip was exciting and somewhat unexpected as I had really thought Matthew was being stupid, but apparently he was on the right track all the time and Sherlock Holmes an' maself were wrong. Some detective team we'd make. It appears that Luke's mum is seeing Mr Chapman from school, which I find unbelievable, but Luke reckons it's all on. He's asked her about it an' she says they are just friends, fellow teachers an' all that shite, but he doesna believe her, particularly after the other night at the cinema. Once he'd grasped the concept that his mum might want to date an' is legally allowed to do what she wants, Luke decided that Chappers wasna so bad, an' for a 'date' his mum could have done worse. This conclusion did take days of therapy from me, patient listener that I am.

So Holmes, the love bird, hatched a plan. A cunning one at that. There was an Open Evening at the college last week, apparently they have one just before

Christmas every year, an' Luke knew both his mum an' Mr Chapman would go as teachers always go to things like that if they get the opportunity, I'm no' sure why 'cos you'd think they would have had enough of it in the day, but it would seem they canny get enough. We decided for the sake of Luke's mum we would go too. The last place you want to go in the evening is to college after you've been there for the day, but for the sake of love an' romance we braved ourselves for the cause.

I was given responsibility for Mr Chapman an' Luke was looking after his mum. Actually old Chappers wasna too bad to talk to an' treated me like an adult. He used to run the photography club at school, which of course I wasna interested in then as it was a school thing, but now that I am it ended up being quite a good conversation.

'What are you doing at college then, Miss Kelman?'

Now normally I would have to be rude an' obnoxious to anyone who called me that an' inform them in snooty tones of ma actual name but Mr Chapman said it in such a nice way that even I couldna take offence. So the first question wasna an interesting start. I have been asked this question so many times, it seems to be the only one adults who don't really know you can come up with. I wish I had a tape recorder so I could press 'play' to reel off my standard answer. The second one was better.

'What do you think of your courses?'

Once I had gone through the explanation I gave to all adults about dropping ma sciences in favour of photography an' theatre studies, we had a decent conversation. In fact I couldna stop maself from gushing with an undignified amount of excitement an' enthusiasm, an' amazingly he was the same. Another photography nut. We were having a real proper conversation an' suddenly he was no longer a teacher, or someone we were trying to pair up with Luke's mum, he was an interesting person an' quite funny in a dry sort of way. I liked him. I think it helped that he never actually taught me properly at school, only on cover lessons when ma science teacher was skiving or had had enough of us. So there was none of that awkwardness you often get when you bump into your old teachers an' not know what to say or what to call them now you've left school.

Luke was guiding his mum carefully around the room, introducing her to his teachers, an' she was stopping to chat to people she knew anyway. I think she was a bit suspicious about Luke and me wanting to be there, and she was even more suspicious when she glanced across the room at me an' saw me chatting to Chappers. As Luke steered her over she was on to our game an' gave both of us the LOOK which meant we were in for it later.

'Mum, this is Mr Chapman, my old science teacher. Ah, but of course you know each other anyway, don't you? That's right, I remember now, you bumped into each other at the cinema. I shall leave you to discuss *Lord of the Rings*. Isla and I were just off to the pub, anyway. Bye Mum, bye Mr Chapman.'

Luke was sooooo going to get it later. He really didna do things by halves. He was really cheeky but funny with it. They both stared at us in disbelief an' I am sure I saw Luke's mum smile as Luke an' I scarpered out of the Refectory an' out into the carpark. You've got to hand it to the boy, he was spot on.

We waited at home for his mum for two hours. She finally turned up, long after the Open Evening had finished. She came straight into the lounge where we were sat. I was slightly nervous actually 'cos I didna know if we had pushed it a wee bit. Maybe she wasna ready to date again yet, maybe she didna even like him at all and we had got it all wrong. But if we had she didna look too angry about it. She sat down an' launched into us.

'That was an interesting stunt, you two. I don't think it was possible for you to have been more obvious, Luke. It could have been very embarrassing for the both of us. I trust you will not meddle in my personal life again, ever.'

This was no' a request but a warning an' I thought we had really blown it until she stopped as she was leaving the room, turned round an' kissed Luke on the head as she said, 'I'm out next Thursday, by the way, so you'll have to fend for yourselves. A friend is taking me out,' and she gave me a wink as she went upstairs. We took it to mean that Mr Chapman had asked her out. I wondered how Luke would feel about this now it was actually happening an no' just a game. I mean if it was me I wouldna be too happy, your teacher, a science teacher at that, going out with your mum, I mean it's just no' right is it, it shouldna be allowed. I wonder what the NSPCC would have to say about it.

LUKE

'I can't believe it's Christmas already, can you, Luke? It seems to come around quicker every time.'

She says this every year as we get out the decorations and put up the cards and plan the big shop, but I don't mind, it's what mums say, isn't it?

'Every year we go to Tesco for the BIG SHOP and the list seems to get longer and more expensive. Doesn't Christmas seem to start earlier each year? I remember seeing cards in the shops in August, for goodness sake.'

She says this every year too.

I'm really looking forward to Matt coming home. I haven't seen him since September, he hasn't been home at all. It pissed me off at first, but then I s'pose he's having such a good time, why would he want to come back to Maidstone? Mum's really excited about seeing him and is planning this huge welcome home thing and making a real deal out of Christmas this year. I haven't told her about Matt's plan for going to

Dad's yet. My dad invited Matt and me for Christmas, which doesn't sound too problematic except my mum loves Christmas, it's her favourite time of year. She hasn't got much family of her own – her parents died when we were really young and her brother Joseph lives in Canada and they aren't close, so Matt and I are all she has and she loves to make a real fuss at this time of year. So how am I supposed to tell her Dad wants to see us too? Matt thinks if we go to Dad's on Boxing Day, then we can spend Christmas Eve and Day with Mum and it'll be OK. That's his motto, 'It'll be OK'. I wish I could think like that.

Mum is in overdrive today 'cos Matt's back tomorrow. She is even cleaning his room. Now this is something I would never attempt, but mums have secretly been on an army training course which initiates them into the ways of the teenage boy so that they don't have to undergo extensive counselling after the event that is ENTERING THE BEDROOM!

Have you ever tried to stop a mother 'cleaning' her offspring's room whilst they are away? DO NOT GO THERE! IT IS DANGEROUS! Everyone knows that the teenager's bedroom is strictly off limits to the parent. There are Keep Out and Give Me My Privacy signs and other suggestions freely hurled at them if they dare to enter this hallowed territory, which they reluctantly respect. Once the teenager is away, however, their room belongs to the mother, she has to 'clean it'. Code for 'snoop', have a good look around, rescue cups and plates lurking under the bed.

When Mum eventually emerges we chat about Matt, fondly and not so fondly, and plan the holidays. I tell her about Dad and his offer, trying not to upset her or put it off or make out like it's a big secret. She looks a bit hurt but reassures me as usual that it's OK.

It must be weird being divorced, having met, fallen in love, got married, had the wedding day, worn the dress, bought the rings, sung hymns, bought a house together, bought cars, gone on holidays, had kids, gone to their school plays together, had countless Christmases together and then you wind up having them apart and sharing your kids over the break with your new partners. Makes you wonder why people do get married, why they would take that chance, because what a huge chance it is. How can you know if it will be OK? If it will work out? Now my mum has to spend Boxing Day on her own and wonder what we are up to at my dad's.

'Don't worry about it, Luke. I have an invite for Boxing Day anyway, which I would have turned down if you two were here, but I don't mind you going to your dad's, honestly. Mr Chapman has invited me to the opera again, so I won't be on my own, if that's what you are worrying about.'

In a previous life she must have been a mind reader – either that or at birth mothers are equipped with special skills enabling them to know the every thought of their children. Bloody hell. I hope she doesn't know my every thought – that could get really embarrassing.

ISLA

Christmas is always problematic. Well, not always, only since Hannah died. Two years ago now. It's gone so slowly. I don't miss her on specific days like her birthday or the anniversary or days when you are supposed to grieve. I miss her for odd reasons, like opening the Advent calender an' having no one to argue with for the chocolate. I remember one year when she opened all of them on the first of December an' scoffed the lot. It took me five days to realise what she had done. I kept hoping the next one would have a wee chocolate hiding behind the door, but no, she'd had them all. I was so sore with her for that, and made her make another one herself with wee penny sweets from the corner shop.

I miss her when Saturday morning telly is on an' there is no one pestering me about coming into town with me an' ma friends, an' no one teasing me about Luke. I miss her when there are only three tooth-brushes in the wee jug in the bathroom, the little things that you would never ever notice when some-one is still there. Teaches you a lesson eh?

It was better this year though, ma mum an' dad actually acknowledging that it was Christmas an' that they could celebrate an' smile an' no' feel guilty for enjoying themselves a little.

They tried really hard on Christmas Day. With a panic they realised they couldna use working in the shop as an excuse to pass the day, so they would have to try. They did try, really hard – they bought pre-sents, made a real dinner, watched the Queen's speech, just for the laughs though, had a dram, an' even played some music. It was OK. Ma dad surprised me the most though. He made me a dark room, out the back of the shop. It used to be the storeroom but they moved stuff around to give me this, the best pre-sent I have ever had, an' it came from ma dad.

'Errr . . . we've seen how hard you've been working on this photo stuff, Isla and, well, your mum thought you might need a room, for all your things so, um, here it is.' Not the best at making speeches ma dad, an' has to pretend it's ma mum's idea. I was so touched that he really seemed to be listening to me at last, an' taking me seriously. What fascinated me even more was that ma mum knew what she was doing. She showed me how to work the room, where to put everything, how much solution I needed to use and basically taught me more over a couple of days than Jim had taught me all term. I had no idea she knew anything about photography.

Jim is ma tutor at college for photography. He is OK but a wee bit annoying, he tries too hard to be liked rather than to teach you. He's Luke's form tutor an' Luke finds him really annoying, he thinks he's a prick. I think that's a bit harsh but then I don't have to have tutor time with him. I can imagine him trying to get them all to 'share their feelings' about everything and 'talk' – a bit of a hippy.

We spent three days in the dark room sorting it all out, an' ma dad would pop down every now an' the while to see how we were 'getting along' an' bring us cups of tea an' biscuits. It was wonderful. Ma mum told me about her dark room when she was a teenager an' how she used to take loads of photos an' had an exhibition once when she was at university.

I was gobsmacked. You think you know your parents so well and that they are just your parents, no more no less, then it turns out they had a life before they had you and did all this amazing stuff. Then they have you, get jobs and stop doing the things they used to. When ma mum showed me her photos, after Dad had gone up the attic an' got down the old crates she kept them in, I felt guilty an' stupid. Guilty because she stopped taking photos once Hannah an' I were needing more of her attention an' stupid 'cos there was me going on about ma course an' showing off for the last term 'cos Jim said I showed promise, an' all the time ma mum knew more than I ever will an' is miles better than me.

We even went through the old albums, of when Hannah and I were little. There were Polaroids of us in bonnets an' little booties, in sandpits, on slides, at school, covered in paint, opening presents at Christmas, ma dad in the background of every one. I'd never noticed before that it was nearly always ma mum behind the camera. It was happy and sad looking at photos of Hannah and finally talking about her a bit, not much, but it's better now than before an' I feel like something has changed with me and ma parents. I'm all they have, apart from each other, an' I kinda get it now.

LUKE

It has to be done. New Year's Eve, where else are you going to be? THE CROWN, of course. Everyone had decided to go there and I mean *everyone*, so getting in was going to prove difficult, but luckily Matt had had the foresight to get in there at opening time this morning and save a good row of trestle tables and stay there all day, securing our space, having a couple of bevvies whilst waiting.

He'd been conscientious enough to get up this morning at eleven and make us all breakfast, which I thought was really nice of him, until I saw the state of the kitchen. I think it fair to say he had used every pot and pan Mum owned, leaving debris, breadcrumbs and smears of egg yolk and milk all over the work top. He had made tea, coffee, juice, toast, croissants and emptied the contents of the fridge into a frying pan and hoped for the best. The result was edible, actually it was really tasty, but the mess he left Mum and I with was incredible. Still, to be fair, the lad had work to do – the pub was open, he had to save tables, and drink pints. Fair enough.

He's actually turned into a good cook since he's been at uni. I guess it's every man for himself there. A diet of toast, curry and Pot Noodles is only going to get you so far. Mum has been teaching him how to cook over the phone. He helped out when we went to Dad's at Christmas. Not that Claire needed much help – she'd already peeled all the vegetables the day before, she is so organised. Two Christmas dinners was definitely a result, even if it did mean having to be polite to her all day, which I was. Her family was there too – her parents, her sister Amy and her husband. I suppose they are my step-family or something complex and P.C. like that.

It wasn't too bad – there was only one contact lens discussion and no mention of a baby. I discreetly had a good look at Claire's stomach – no signs of a bump so I think we are safe. I did notice a bottle of folic acid tablets though. Now I know it's not only pregnant women who take these but it did get me concerned and give me something to keep my eye on in the future. Anyway, I preferred Christmas Eve and Day with Mum and Matt and am definitely looking forward to the pub later.

As we walk into The Crown I can tell the mood is good. Everyone is home from uni or celebrating their last day or two before having to return to work or college. That's one of the main reasons I stayed on at college, to avoid having to get a job. The thought of having to go to work every day, having to get up or someone might fire you, having to be somewhere on time five days a week with only the weekend off, is horrific. College seemed a more sensible option. How I pity those office workers at the bar who are still in their suits and ties. Surely they can't have been working on NEW YEAR'S EVE???? It's inhumane. Maybe they just don't have any clothes other than their office attire or perhaps they are trapped in their suits and can't get out. Either way, they are certainly letting their hair down now. The jackets are off and ties are being thrown across the bar and co-workers are checking out each other's tonsils, something to make a resolution about tomorrow morning, for the New Year.

Matt beckons Isla and me over and we squeeze ourselves through the mass of people and shout our orders to those who have succeeded in their expedition to the bar. The final task that awaits them is to catch the barmaid's eye, not an easy feat when she is pointedly ignoring most of the rabble and serving the select chosen few. Tricky ladies, barmaids – you can only speak to them if they address you first and then they have to judge if you are fit to have a conversation with. If they work out that you are not eighteen yet, God help you. I have got away with it so far.

Andrew James didn't help when we came in here to celebrate my seventeenth. He shouted/screamed/belched 'Happy birthday' to me and when the barmaid asked how old I was, we had to gaffer tape his mouth shut to prevent him from giving the whole thing away. Jamesy raises his pint to me and winks whilst taking a good look at Isla, leering pointlessly at her. He's fancied her since she came to England but luckily stands no chance. I wink back at him, whilst Isla rolls her heavily made-up eyes. She's gone for it tonight – the short skirt, hair up and lots of make-up on. She looks bloody gorgeous and I'm not looking too bad myself in my favourite T-shirt and jeans which I had to rescue from my mum's dry-cleaning bag – she really doesn't get jeans.

We settle in next to one another and listen to Matt hold court with Ripper and the rest of the skinny, malnourished students who have returned home firstly to be fed up by the parents then to be driven to the pub. Later they will walk/stagger/crawl home after telling tales of their adventures and exploits at university. Isla and I tune in.

'Yeah, but the best night was the toga party when that girl's breasts fell out of her sheet and she was so pissed she didn't even notice till I asked her if I could have a nibble!' Ripper seemed to be telling tales that mostly involved women's breasts and his lack of real contact with them.

'No way! The best was when we had a lock-in in The Shakespeare and Smithy fell off the bar after he'd been dancing with those girls, remember the ones who threw their bras at him, and he lost his balance and fell over. The ambulance men were really arsey with us and gave me a right lecture, which I couldn't concentrate on 'cos I was trying to focus but all I could see were the flashing lights.' Sounds like lots of alcohol at play and more mention of women, their breasts and underwear. I can't wait to go to uni.

'You've got to come and stay, Luke. We're moving out of halls, well, we've been chucked out, but we've got a house and you can come and kip on my floor and we'll go out.' Another proposal from Matt but this time I am going. It sounds really good, not just the breasts bit.

We've been here three hours now and I can't feel my legs any more and it's not cramp. Isla has done her usual party trick of drinking too much too quickly and has fallen asleep in the corner. Shedded, mashed, rendered, twisted, trolleyed, legless, wrecked, Brahms and Liszt (pissed), trashed, steaming, tanked, wasted – so many different words to describe most of the pub, including me. I will regret this in the morning, but no time to worry about that now – another tequila slammer is on its way down to me and then it's the final countdown.

'FIVE, FOUR, THREE, TWO, ONE, HAPPY NEW YEAR!!!!!!!!!!!'

Isla wakes up in time for a kiss and then passes out in my arms. Happy New Year.

ISLA

I have never had a two-dayer before but I suppose after New Year's Eve is when you are going to get one. I'd heard the rumours and thought it was another urban myth but no, I can confirm the banging in ma head is still there, the sick queasy feeling in ma stomach is threatening to rise up out of ma throat an' I canny tolerate the smell of food. A two-day hangover, ugh! I never thought I'd be unlucky enough to get one, I am such a lightweight. It wasna even worth it 'cos I canny remember much after eleven. I have a blurry recollection of coats an' wanting to lie down. Oh God, I was so worried I'd made an arse of maself until Luke rang an' told me I was OK an' just fell asleep as usual. I wish I wouldna do that but I get carried away an' drink more than I should an' then I get sleepy.

I get so excited when we are off for a big night out an' do all the right things like eat bread an' drink milk to line ma tummy an' I try an' pace maself but I think

I am just destined to be a lightweight. Oh God, I can remember hiccups. Oh the shame! I bet I was twisted, it certainly feels like I was. I went for a walk yesterday to clear ma head an' hope fresh air would be reviving or have some pure qualities which might filter into ma knackered body. I took ma camera with me in case I got inspired. I'd seen this competition I wanted to enter, for photography, *The Sunday Times* Amateur Photographer of the Year. To enter you couldna have had anything published before, well I had no problems there. I wanted ma mum to enter too but at the same time I didna in case she proved too steep competition – not that she'd enter anyway. She wasn't as interested in ma photos as she has been, gone a bit cold on the topic, I didna know why.

I walked for about half an hour before realising that nothing was going to get rid of ma hangover an' I was too worried about what I'd done the night before. I hate that feeling, when you wake up an' instantly flashes of the night before come back to haunt you an' tease you with half-memories of what you might have done or said, but you can't be sure. So you lie there all day, waiting for someone to ring you to tell you what happened before you can venture out into the world.

I decided to walk round to Luke's to see how he was

faring. He was on much better form than me, though he normally is. I think men have a higher tolerance of alcohol – either that or him an' his brother have hollow legs. They both looked fine, sat watching TV and arguing happily over the remote control.

'Where's your mum, then?' I asked as I collapsed on to the sofa next to Luke, who was looking far too well an' healthy next to ma pallor.

'Out with Mr Chapman. They went to the ballet last night and are out having lunch today. OOOoooohhh!' Luke felt compelled to make a childish noise whenever he talked about his mum an' her romance, in the manner of a child in the playground. I think it made the whole thing less real an' threatening for him.

'So you've met him then, Matt. What do you think?' It was hard work tearing either of them away from James Bond and I didna want to watch, it always reminds me of Hannah. I used to call her Bond as she was always spying on me and annoying me. I'd love her to be here now, annoying me, telling Mum an' Dad what I'm up to. Matt finally answers ma question, dragging his eyes away from the telly.

'Mmm yep. He's all right, sound bloke – shame he's a teacher but they've got loads in common then, I s'pose. Yourself? Looking a bit rough there, Jock.'

How amusing an' original his nickname for me was. Never heard that one before. Smug bugger, looking fine himself, not a hangover in sight, empty Microchip boxes an' crisp packets littering the table in front of them both.

'So last night then . . . it was good?' I needed to do ma insecure checking thing with Luke as ma memory had once again failed me.

'Yes, top night. Although you missed most of it from eleven onwards, little pass-out Queen. Awwww, you all right? Feeling a bit sensitive? Want to come up to my chamber of lurve?'

How could he joke around an' laugh so LOUDLY, when ma head was doing a fine impression of a brass band all by itself an' ma stomach was auditioning for the circus by cart-wheeling around ma insides? I wanted Luke to maself suddenly. I nodded an' we went up to his room.

We were sat on the bed for about three seconds before Luke jumped me. I was surprised as he's normally a bit funny about messing around when Matt or his mum are in the house, but he didna seem bothered this time. I was starting to feel a wee bit better – the healing power of his kisses, no doubt. It was proving really difficult to get any time on our own, as none of our parents would let us sleep in the same house together with their 'not under our roof'-type statements. Actually I hadn't braved the question with ma dad as I knew the proposition could put him in hospital, such would be the shock that his daughter might be having sex. Admittedly, no' much sex, but definitely occasionally, grabbed chances at house parties or the odd time when one of our homes was empty of the parents, not often.

This seemed a prime opportunity, with Matt so engrossed in James Bond, Luke's mum out for lunch and, well, we couldn't waste such a chance. Luke was definitely different since we had moved to this stage of our relationship, he was more affectionate an' complimentary, but sometimes he could also be a wee bit presumptuous. Now that we were having sex he seemed to think we should be having it all the time, which I didna want, yet.

But obviously sometimes it was good to seize the opportunity an' go for it, an' go for it we did – clothes came off, magazines were chucked off the bed, crisp packets removed from under the pillow, music switched on and passion ensued. When you are in the middle of sex you are concentrating an' wrapped up in the moment, only really aware of the person you are with, unless it's really bad sex and then I suppose you might be aware of cars outside, what time it is, what you might be having for your tea later. I'd heard women gossiping in the shop about how they compiled their shopping lists while lying back an' thinking of England. I hoped I would never do this or ever get to that stage with a man.

I was lucky that Tesco did not enter ma head when I was with Luke an' I hoped he were thinking about me an' not Sainsbury's. What we were definitely not thinking about was what time it was or that his mum was stood in the doorway with her jaw wide open and her face contorted into a mask of horror. I imagine a mum doesn't really want to see her teenage son's naked bottom at all, but to be confronted with this naked bottom moving in rhythm with a girl underneath it is far too much information, an assault on the senses of a mother. I cannot even begin to put into words how unbelievably embarrassed I was. No one has seen me naked since I was ten, apart from Luke an' Hannah when she walked in on me in the bath once.

I couldna believe this was happening to me, to us, in his mum's house. I thought I would crumple up into a ball an' never move again. Oh my God, ma stomach is turning at the memory an' it was only yesterday.

It was so awful that no one could speak, least of all me with Luke lying on top of me. Then, jumping up out of bed an' grabbing a pair of pants to cover his modesty, the first word that came into Luke's head was 'Mum!' Well that much was obvious, but by this time she had left an' shut the door behind her without a word. What word was there that could have made this gut-crunching-nails-dragging-down-a-blackboard feeling of utter shame and embarrassment any better? It was beyond awful. We sat on the bed, slowly dressing, without uttering a word. The most natural act in the world had us hanging our heads in the deepest embarrassment. Why *were* we so embarrassed? It was only sex, we told each other, but in his mum's house it's like swearing in church or farting loudly in a library. Just not the done thing. But we had done it an' now we had to deal with it, but how? What could we possibly say?

LUKE

'I am so sorry, Mum.'

'Luke, you can stop apologising, you know. You've been saying sorry all week. It's OK.'

I know it isn't OK and I know we have to talk about it but she has been waiting for Matt to go back to uni. I have been waiting all week for her to come and talk to me, tell me off, get cross, give me the LOOK, say how I'd let her down. Anything would be better than the silence and the small talk and the not mentioning 'it'. God, this has got to be the worst scenario possible. Your mum walking in on you and your girlfriend mid-shag, seeing your arse bobbing up and down and maybe worse when you stupidly jump up butt naked!

I feel sick, I don't know what with, but I just want to forget the whole bloody thing and until she says something I am trapped in purgatory wondering what she's going to say. I feel like I have definitely overstepped the mark. I've never really done anything to upset my mum before, never got in real trouble at school, never been brought home by the police, although Mum once threatened to take me to the police for shoplifting. I was five at the time, Tesco was the scene of the crime. The object of my desire was a pink felt-tip pen in a pack of thirty pens, placed cunningly by the checkout next to the sweets – really unfair on mums, doing that, but then it's a consumerist world. Anyway I wanted that pink pen – no, *needed* it, desired it, craved it, but I already had a felt-tip set at home and Mum was not caving in to my demands, so I waited until she was busy loading the shopping on to the conveyor belt and reached into the packet, took the pink pen, placed it in my pocket and went home. Whilst enjoying myself later on, trying to keep within the strict lines of my colouring-in book, my mum spied the pink pen in my little clenched fist and extracted a confession within tear-stained seconds. She even managed to convince me that the police knew about it and the only way she could stop them coming round to talk to me was for me to swear never ever to steal anything again. It worked. I was terrified.

So this, this thing with Isla, is the first real, serious, semi-adult thing I have done that could have annoyed her. I can stand it no longer. I am going to talk to her.

'Mum, about the other afternoon, you know when . . .'

She is not making this easy for me, peering at me over the rim of her glasses above her newspaper. I am having difficulty with my vocabulary again.

'You know when Isla and I were in my . . . umm . . . room?'

She picks up on the pleading tone in my voice. 'When you were having sex in the middle of the afternoon, in my house, whilst I stood in the doorway, after having called out your name and knocked on the door. That afternoon, Luke?'

Ah, sarcasm. This is apparently the lowest form of wit. I am certainly feeling low when it is put like that. Where to go now? Try another apology I think.

'Um . . . I am really . . . we are really sorry. Isla is so embarrassed, she can't even come round now. Mum, please don't be mad?' I really don't know what to say, what is there to say?

'You are missing the point, Luke. If you are embarrassed about it, you shouldn't be having sex. You shouldn't be acting like an adult if you can't take responsibility for what you are doing. The fact that Isla feels she can't come here or face me or whatever suggests you are both far too immature for a sexual

146

relationship. You could have made a baby the other day, you know that, don't you? Don't give me the wounded puppy look. Are you ready for the possibility of having a child, being tied to one another for the rest of your lives? Are you ready to make a grandchild for Mr and Mrs Kelman? No, I thought not. If you haven't thought about these possibilities, what are you doing?'

She is really scaring me. I haven't thought about all of this 'cos I have been enjoying myself, I am glad we are having sex at all, I am not going to ruin it with talk about babies and scary stuff. It is difficult enough talking about condoms, pausing to put one on, taking it off at the end and dealing with it. The whole thing is so undignified that to introduce the fear factor into the equation would put us both off altogether.

'Are you using more than one form of contraception? I am presuming you are not so stupid as to use nothing at all?'

Huh, the cheek!

'Of course we are. Condoms.' I mumble the last bit as you don't really want to talk about condoms with your mum, do you?

' . . . And?'

What does she mean, 'and'? What does the woman want, blood?

'Just condoms. Why?' Now she has me worried. What does she know that I don't, apart from a hell of a lot by the tone of her voice.

'Do you check afterwards if they have split? Do you check if they are in date? Do you know how effective they are against pregnancy and disease?'

What is this, the Spanish Inquisition? Check if they've split? Surely they are tested for all that. And how can a condom go out of date – it's not exactly food is it, although the chocolate-flavoured ones seem to sell well. Anyway, this is too much.

'No, but no one does stuff like that, do they.' Well, I don't anyway and I can't see my mates reading the box looking for the little use-by date stamped on, or even printed on the condom itself.

'Well, people who don't want an STI or a baby do and so should you. You need to sort yourselves out, both of you. Do you know why your dad and I got married? Because I was four months pregnant with Matthew. Not because we were soul mates or destined to be together. My parents would have died of shame if we hadn't. You are not just having fun here, Luke, you are playing with real, live consequences. I've never regretted Matt for a moment but I wish I had waited, I wish I had thought about it all more. I wish someone had told me the options. I am not mad with you, I am not even angry. I am just worried that neither of you is really thinking about what you are doing, other than enjoying the moment, which is fine if you have protected yourselves, but you haven't, not properly. You need to sort yourselves out and behave like adults instead of playing at it.'

And with that she leaves me, terrified at the prospect of an STI, a baby and a very angry Mr and Mrs Kelman.

ISLA

It does look beautiful even if I say so maself. I spent ages perfecting it, choosing a lovely pattern and arrangement of little codes and symbols, and the colour scheme is an interior designer's dream. It's a shame I haven't left much time to actually use it, to put ma beautiful revision plan to any use an' do some revision. At least the subjects are narrowed down now to theatre studies, English an' photography, no' like at GCSE when you have to do pointless things like maths an' design. I made an elephant in design, out of wood. It took me most of the term, if no' the year, an' when I handed it to Mr Calster the bloody trunk snapped off in his hand an' I got an E! It's no' ma fault if the man's hands were too big.

Revision is a torture device invented by someone who loathes the human race. I spent all of the weekend revising, no' going out once, no' even on Saturday night which felt really weird, 'cos since I was thirteen Saturday night has been something exciting, something to anticipate for the whole week. In fact I canny remember spending a Saturday night in once I'd worked out what Saturday nights were all about. Up to the age of thirteen I was under the foolish an' often common misapprehension that Saturday nights were spent with your parents, watching TV, playing games, being a family, then I hit thirteen and realised they were for getting away from your parents and instead involved seeing your friends, going out, bowling, ice-skating, cinema and then, once make-up was properly applied in an effort to look eighteen, pubs and clubs were frequented.

So to spend a Saturday night at home, with the parents, but revising, was odd to say the least. In a way I had enforced the whole staying-in thing as punishment to maself as I was still too embarrassed to go to Luke's an' I couldna be arsed to make the effort to go to The Crown without him.

I was still really flustered about his mum walking in on us. She was all right with me but insisted I go and get the pill from the doctors an' tell ma mum an' dad. I thought she was raving to suggest such a thing, I think ma dad would consider assassinating Luke if he knew what we were up to. Not that there is anything wrong with it, it's just I am still ten years old in his eyes. He canny accept the fact that I am a woman, an adult, well I like to kid maself I am.

It's ironic, but the more I behave like a kid, no' taking responsibility for the whole sex thing, the more ma mum an' dad are actually treating me like a real person, instead of an extension of themselves. I know Mrs Field would never tell them about what happened, but they seem to be so much better with me lately. It sounds bizarre but I think the dark room has helped, they have accepted that I am mad keen on photography an' no' playing at it.

I've entered the competition – well, I have filled in the form, which is the easy part. I've got to submit a photo but I know it has to be good, original, interesting an' catch the judges' eye. It canny be another sunset, or a wee baby laughing, or someone fishing on a lake, it's all been done, clichés. I so want to be original, to be a success, for someone to say, 'Wow, you have got talent' an' pay me to be a photographer an' make ma dreams come true. Ma dad thinks I am a dreamer but ma mum has started saying why can't I have dreams? If we don't have dreams we are soulless, a robot, cruising on autopilot through life, a pointless existence, an' that our dreams see us through. I agree with her. If it wasna for photography I would be just another someone, just another wee sixteen-year-old making her way through college, having a boyfriend, wearing make-up, trying to grow ma hair, trying not to get pregnant, drinking too much – just another story, another average existence. I don't want to be average.

Ma mum comes in to help me once in the while an' sometimes we talk whilst we are waiting for the photos to develop – no' much, just little bits about Hannah, or Luke or school or her an' ma dad. We'll say 'Remember the time when . . . ' an' laugh an' it helps so much to know that these conversations will happen again an' it's no' going to be silence, moods, dark looks, things hidden away, private bags, secret things put up in the attic so we can pretend Hannah dying never happened, an' just watch TV with the sound turned down at three in the morning 'cos we canny sleep for the thoughts whirring incessantly in our lonely heads.

It's just little things that show me that Mum is OK, that she is no' trapped in the house any more. She has made some friends, somewhere, an' she meets them once a week an' comes back smiling an' looks like she has done a good thing by leaving the house, has shift-ed some of the weight. I watch her going out once a week, when there was a time when she didna leave the house for a month. Now she waves 'Bye', out with ma dad to meet some friends they've made, an' I am so proud I feel like the parent, like the adult. Sometimes.

LUKE

I am not having any luck with this whole revision lark. I don't know that I want to go to uni anyway. I reckon most people go because they don't know what else to do, unless you are a brain like my brother then you need further study to keep you going or you will shrivel up and combust. I am not a brain. I don't think I suit this whole education system. I should have done a trade, gone off to college one day a week out of school with the 'special people'. These were the ones at school who couldn't cope or the school couldn't cope with them and they would be released once a week into freedom. We used to take the piss but they are actually the ones who are earning money now and doing jobs they like, unlike penniless me still stuck in a classroom. I want to be out there, travelling or whatever, seeing more of the world than another white board with the teacher's impression of spaghetti projectile-vomited all over it in an attempt at handwriting. I am bored.

My mum used to get really cross with us if we said we were bored when we were little. She would make us tidy up our rooms or paint or read a story, which made it worse, 'cos you want someone to feel sorry for you, you don't want them to come up with a solution to the problem which involves you having to deal with the situation. You want escapism. That's what I want, escapism. I'm going to see if my mum has got any.

'Mum, I'm bored and I don't want to do any more revision. Can we go out? Let's go to the cinema, we could catch the eight o'clock showing.' Escapism in the form of the BIG SCREEN, can't beat it and I know Isla won't come as she's revising, which is all she's done this whole month, it seems.

'Oh, I'd love to, but I am already going out.'

Pardon?

'WHAT? With whom, may I ask?' My mum does not go out on a school night, she has marking to do and preparing the next day's lessons and cutting up verbs on little bits of paper and making games. She's one of those teachers who bother. So to hear she is going out on a Wednesday night is unheard of.

'With Mr Chapman, um . . . we're going to the cinema, actually. Do you want to come? I'm sure he wouldn't mind . . .'

Hmmm . . . to play gooseberry or not to play gooseberry? I cannot stand being at home one minute longer but I have not plunged so low that I could stoop to go out with my mum and her . . . 'boyfriend'? too undignified, 'friend'? too innocent, 'lover'? cannot think about that . . . so 'him', Mr Chapman – not offensive, not annoying, perfectly fine as blokes go but I just don't want to go with them on their date. It would be too much. So I will have to decline without hurting my mum's feelings. This could be tricky . . .

'Sorry, Mum, but I really should get on with the revision, I was just being lazy. You have a good time.' Kind, thoughtful, and the mention of revision should let her down gently.

'OK, great!' And she bounces off upstairs, presumably to do something as teenage-like as 'get ready'. She seemed to take that really well, on the whole, though clearly she's upset that I am not going with her and is covering up by being light and bubbly. What a mum! Well, if she is going out then I shall have to entertain myself by ringing up Isla and disturbing her revision. To the batphone!

'Hello, can I speak to Isla, please?' I hate it when I get her dad. He always makes me feel like I am asking the earth.

'No, she's revising.' Ah, you are her keeper, are you, and cannot let her have a break and speak to her beloved.

'Well, I won't keep her long.' That's what I tell you anyway.

'Isla! ISLA! Phone.' Such beautiful manners for such a pleasant man, and what a wonderful conversationalist he is too.

'Hello?'

That's better, one Kelman I do want to speak to. 'Hi, it's me. How you doing? I cannot be arsed with this whole revision thing. Want to come and lead me astray? My mum has gone out so I am all alone . . .' How subtle I am.

'No. I mean I can't, I've got loads more to do and I have said I'm staying in tonight.' What? Refusal? Unbelievable. She cannot resist me, surely.

'Come on, I'll even cook you pizza? We can get a video out and chill? Or go down The Crown?' So many offers, she is sure to choose one.

'All right, give me half an hour to finish this last bit and convince ma parents you are no' Satan's spawn and I'll be over, but I don't want to stay in. I'm bored with staying in. Let's go to the pub? I'll bring my camera in case anything takes ma eye or something of interest happens – you never know, even in Maidstone something must happen sometimes.'

Success. She has succumbed to my charms, well the lure of alcohol and a possible photo, anyway. Half an hour to waste, the computer beckons and a Bud to keep me going. I feel a big night coming on. If my mum is out on a school night then I had better follow her lead.

ISLA

I have never seen him so drunk. I don't think I have seen anyone, anywhere, ever, so drunk, except ma Uncle Ben an' he's an alcoholic who lives in what ma dad refers to as 'a bothy' off the West Coast so you canny count him. But Luke, I was amazed an' totally humiliated for him an' for me. He went on about how unhappy he was at college an' all that but I just thought that was revision talking or the drink, then once he lost the ability to talk at all I got worried.

We went to The Crown, as usual, an' bumped into Andrew James an' a couple of others from school who are all working now. Andrew is a painter an' decorator an' making good money. He looked really well an' happy, even if his brother was a mad bam pot. Well, Luke an' him got talking an' Luke was almost convinced he should join Andrew in his business until banshee-girl Georgia Hopkins fluttered her way across the room an' practically sat on Luke's lap, while informing him about her wonderful new job in telesales, which, correct me if I am mistaken, is just ringing people up an' convincing them to buy something which I am sure they would have already bought if they really wanted it. Telesales ma arse. Anyway, Luke was sold an' thought this was the way to his first million. He drank in her lies an' charm an' talk of commission as he drank in more and more Stella. I let Luke carry on 'cos there is nothing more annoying than a girlfriend telling her boyfriend he has had enough or should stop drinking. I've seen the arguments it can cause an' the looks of pity from other blokes when this scene takes place so I refused to be that girl, even when Luke started slurring his words an' talking about going into business with Andrew James one moment an' then on the next pint he was definitely going to ring Georgia's boss on Monday an' see if they had any telesales vacancies. If someone had suggested to Luke that night that he become a pole-dancer I think he would have considered it – in fact he would probably have given us a demonstration, he was so pissed.

I was embarrassed watching him as he remembered who I was an' lurched over to me, slinging his arm around me, leaning in for a sloppy kiss as his eyes slipped in and out of focus, talking to me very loudly whilst looking over my shoulder. I was not impressed.

Things got worse when it came to closing time. Suddenly no one seemed so entertained by Luke's antics an' ramblings any more, they had homes to go to an' I was left with a six-foot-one no-longer-skinny bloke to get into a taxi an' home. But . . .

'There'ssss no way I's going home yet, 'ss fun to be had an' kebabs, the laws of alch–, alchol, aclcholo says that you must DRINK! An' eat kebabs!' He had been like this for the last hour, mostly talking a fine brand of arse at the top of his voice, boring anyone who was listening, mostly me. So to the kebab shop we went an' then on to a bench for Luke to eat an' hopefully sober up.

It was whilst we were on the bench that I had the best idea. I had taken ma camera with me to the pub as I had hoped I might be inspired – you never knew, someone might have a fight (they did, over a bag of peanuts, it was boring) or there might be a scene of romance (there was, between the bar man and the landlady, but the landlord was upstairs, so I couldn't document that) or an accident could happen (it did, the landlord came downstairs mid-snog), but there had been nothing that had caught ma interest until now when I looked over at the love of ma life, slumped on the bench, kebab all down his front an' round his mouth, a can of Stella clutched firmly in his hand an' a wide drunken smile across his face. I got ma Canon out an' snapped, just once, an' quickly, as I wanted to take it before I decided it was unfair. This was the one, I would send it off tomorrow just in time to meet the closing date of the competition. I also wanted to show Luke in the morning what he looked like an' what an arse he had been all night an' how he needed to sort himself out. Not that I am a nagging girlfriend, o'course.

We finally convinced a taxi driver to take us home after guaranteeing that Luke would not puke an' if he did he would pay for the cleaning. After all that we finally rolled up outside his house at one o'clock in the morning – a perfect time if you are very drunk to start singing at the top of your voice, very badly, out of tune.

'We wiiisshhhhh yewwww a merry Chrrrismmmas an' a 'appy new yeeaaaarrrrr!' An odd choice for the time of year, an' sung so badly it was barely recognis-able. I hung ma head in shame as I tried to shove Luke towards the front door, rummaging in his pock-ets for the keys, whilst cursing him under ma breath. I was praying his mum was a heavy sleeper an' would no' open her window to see what was going on. Unfortunately she was just pulling up with Mr Chapman as we were about to open the front door. She got out and slammed the car door shut, shouting goodnight to him (he looked a little hurt), an' then she informed me she would take care of things from here, hailed me a taxi, and shoved Luke rather firmly inside the house.

LUKE

I knew I had failed, but I didn't tell anyone. You know how people always come out of exams saying to anyone who will listen, 'Oh, I've *so* failed, I really messed that up, I am going to have to re-sit, blah, blah, blah,' then they pass with flying colours and laugh and say 'Gosh! I really thought I'd failed'. Yeah yeah, you big liars.

I knew I had so I didn't bother with all the pretence and bollocks of going on about it. I told my mum and she believed me and said it didn't surprise her, seeing as I had done no revision. Huh! The cheek! I had done some, just not enough. I think I am going to have to leave college. I've got a meeting with 'Call me Jim 'cos I am a seventies throwback' form tutor in three minutes. Grrrrrrr. I answer my mobile as I wait outside his room. It's Isla.

'Hello?'

'Hi, guess what? I won! I BLOODY WON! I CAME FIRST! ME! I DID. OH MY GODDDDD!'

She is somewhat excitable and very loud, screaming down my ear.

'You've won what?' As I utter these famous last words I remember what she is going on about, but it is too late. I have sealed my fate, she will return to those words for ever and use them with skill in any future argument. I can hear it already, 'Do you remember the time when you forgot about my competition?'

'MY PHOTOGRAPHY competition, for God's sake, Luke!'

Uh oh. In trouble now, make up for it quickly, think of something wonderful to say.

'That's great, Isla. Well done! Shall we go to the cinema to celebrate? No, look, I'll take you out for a meal?' This seems better from the reply I get.

'OK, tonight? An' it has to be a surprise where and can it not be a Beefeater or a Harvester, please? A proper restaurant? OK, bye, ring me later, love you!' As she rings off, Jim's door opens and hordes of frightened-looking Year 13s come scurrying out, muttering under their breath 'He's a nutter' and 'Bloody terrifies me'. Great!

'Come in, come in, dude. Enter do. Greetings and salutations!'

What??

Jim sits down on his chair and throws his legs up on to the table in front of him with such a swing that he nearly falls backwards off his chair. I try very hard not to laugh. It ends up coming out as a snort instead. He gives me a cross look.

'Look, Luke, this isn't a laughing matter, mate. You have messed up, your results were shit, to be fair, and now there's this concern over the photo and I have got people asking awkward questions and there's talk of you having to leave or re-sit. What's going on, man?'

Wow, he just launched into that one. What is he on about? I know my results were bad, that wasn't a surprise – well not to me anyway – but what photo? Oh God, have they found my Britney stash? They are only photos out of a newspaper. Admittedly she is baring all, but hey, it was her choice. I just keep them at the bottom of my bag, or maybe they got into one of my essay pockets. Oh shit!

'Um sir . . . sorry, Jim, what are you talking about? What umm photos?' I brace myself for his reply, expecting his disgust to be plastered across his face.

'Luke, you do know what I am talking about, don't you? Have you been in the entrance hall? The exhibition of the winners of *The Sunday Times* competition? We had one winner and five runners-up out of MY class!' He looks so smug. His class. Well, I still don't get it. What's it got to do with me?

'What's it got to do with me?'

He is looking rather strangely in disbelief at me. I wish he would bloody tell me.

'I think you ought to go and see for yourself, Luke,' he says, with a grave nodding of the head, so full of wisdom is Jim, so full of shit. What a waste of ten minutes. I get up and leave, meaning to go home, but as I walk to the bus stop several people stare. I wonder if I have got something down my T-shirt or if my hair is a mess – nothing new there though. I consider the possibility that I am suddenly a sex magnet but have to quickly discount this when people start sniggering. Right, I'd better go and look at these photos and try and work out how they are linked to whatever Jim was going on about.

As I walk into the entrance hall, a hush falls over the group of people gathered around the display stands. One bloke shouts at me, raising his fist, 'Well done, mate, looks top!' What?

I edge nearer the stands. The winner's photo is in the middle and I am quite excited as I look at the title

'CLOSING TIME' and see ISLA KELMAN underneath the photo. The photo is of . . . me. Enlarged, huge, blown-up beyond belief me. On a bench somewhere with something in my hand. I peer closer and see a can of beer in my right hand and what looks like the remains of a kebab in the other, most of which is plastered all over my face and T-shirt. I look so pissed. A complete tosser sat on a bench somewhere grinning stupidly at the camera. At Isla's camera. She took this and sent it. I turn round and walk out of the entrance hall, with everyone's eyes burning into my back.

ISLA

We've been split up for nearly a month now. I can remember when all I could think about was Luke an' would he want me, would he fancy me, what if he kissed me, then what would happen after he kissed me, would he want to sleep with me, would he be embarrassed the next day, would we go to college together, would we maybe get married later an' have kids an' all that stuff? I did think we would always be together an' now we're not. I pushed it too far. It's ma fault, I know, an' I've said sorry an' everything but it's all too late according to him, or his mum, who we are communicating through. How childish.

I always thought, an' I realise now it was arrogant, that I had the upper hand in the whole relationship thing, that it was me who called the shots, an' it was, until I blew it. I feel so awful. I was so mad at him for getting drunk an' being an arse an' flirting with stupid banshee-girl who ignored me at school 'cos I was the new girl from Scotland an' I never made friends with her or any of them. It had never mattered 'cos I had Luke, but now I have no one.

I've got friends in ma classes now. Laurie in English lit is lovely an' there's Sam in photography an' that but it's not the same. I blew it an' I deserve Luke being mad at me but the whole not talking to me thing, an' not taking ma calls, an' telling his mum to say he's out, is a wee bit of a shock. I didna think he had it in him to be mean.

It wasn't just the drunken evening that made me do it, it was the fact that I knew it made a good photo, the one of Luke pissed. It was thoughtless to send it in, to try an' win at his expense but I really wanted it. I haven't wanted to win anything before. I've always avoided competitions of all kinds; sports days, poetry, art, singing, dancing, swimming – I have never been interested but this, photography, I really wanted an' I didna stop to think how he'd feel. I know it's no excuse but I didna realise the college would make a display of the photos for all to see, including Luke an' his mum. I thought he would never see it an' I would get away with it an' ma revenge would be exacted without hurting him. That's what really hurts me an' makes me feel sick, that I have hurt him. I've spent most of ma time worrying that he might hurt me, I

171

didna think I would end up being the one in the wrong.

His mum must be really pissed off at me too. God, I don't think I'll ever be able to go round there again. Ma mum an' dad are mad with me too an' we were getting on so well. I never thought I'd hear ma dad stick up for Luke. He's normally 'that Luke' or 'your hhhhm hhhm boyfriend' with the words sticking in his throat.

'You must have known that he would see it at some point, love?' Ma mum with the softer touch.

'She didna think, did she? Just went on straight ahead an' did what she wanted to, as usual, without even thinking about the consequences. Poor wee sod, I canny say I blame him for dumping you.' Cheers, Dad, summing up ma behaviour rather well this time as it happens. I knew all he was saying was true so I had nothing to say.

'What are you going to do about it?'

Good question. I had no idea. I seemed to be lurching from one disaster to the next at the moment an' I thought I was so sorted 'cos I had passed ma exams so well. I felt so smug and a bit superior to Luke 'cos he had failed an' deserved to. I am such a bad person, no wonder he doesna want to go out with me any more. I wouldna want to go out with me. Ma mum an' dad had looked like they were really surprised at the depths their daughter had plunged to. Exploiting her boyfriend to win a competition. An' the worst thing was that they were right, which is sickening, as you never really want to admit that there is the possibility that your parents could be . . . right!

I was in ma room for hours before I came up with a solution to the end of the world as I knew it. I played ma music for hours. I lay on ma bed an' looked at photos of Luke an' me, cinema tickets, the programme from a musical the school had taken us to see in London, a menu from Dave's Deli where we used to work, Luke's e-mail address on a little card he had given me, his old trainers which I had wanted to keep for some mad reason which I couldna remember now but I had the grace to feel embarrassed by.

I had a poem clutched in ma hand that I had written for him – not on Valentine's Day, as one would expect, but on the second anniversary of Hannah's death. The poem said more than I could ever say.

I walked to college quicker than I ever had before, causing ma toes to blister, but it was no less than I deserved. In fact I welcomed the pain. It took ma mind off how awful and selfish I was feeling. I marched into college after persuading the cleaner an' the caretaker to just let me in for one minute before locking up, an' I swiftly took ma photo down, ripped it into shreds and threw it into the bin. The cleaner emptied it with a bemused expression on his face as if to say 'Kids today! Crazy, eh?'

As I was still standing there, he came over to the display stands with a suspicious look on his face to see what I was up to. When he saw what I had replaced ma photo with he smiled an' patted me on the shoulder, which made me feel worse as I trudged home, ma little toe bleeding all the way.

LUKE

I am fed up with people staring at me still. Everywhere I go, people are looking and whispering, or at least it feels that way. Paranoia is a powerful thing. I wish it were all over or had never happened. My own fault for getting so pissed I suppose, but you don't expect your girlfriend to take advantage and humiliate you in front of the whole bloody college, do you?

That's what I can't forgive her for. That she could do that to me after all we've been through, and I thought we'd been getting on so well lately. I am glad I dumped her. I have never dumped anyone before Isla, I have never had the opportunity. It's funny though, I don't really feel that good about it. As the dumper, surely I should be glad of my decision and feel I have done what any man would do in the situation? I should be out on the town, getting off with lots of girls to get over the whole thing. I definitely shouldn't be feeling guilty, or depressed, or sad, or mopey, or wondering have I been too harsh. NO! I haven't! Even my mum thinks it was a low blow, and she loves Isla.

I'd better get the daily torture and humiliation over with and walk through the entrance hall to my first lesson. I wish there was another way to get to media studies but it's next to the entrance hall, just my luck. Great. Even more crowds than usual, more mockery to come my way. I glance at the display stands as I walk past. I can't help it, I've been doing it nearly every day for a month, it reminds me how mad I am at her if my resolve weakens and I consider taking one of her phone calls.

For the first time in weeks I am not greeted with my drunken and debauched image staring back at me, magnified. I am looking at a sheet of paper on which is scrawled Isla's messy handwriting. What? Someone has taken my photo down and put up . . . a . . . poem, the poem Isla wrote for me. How did they get hold of that? She must have done it, but why? People move away as I lean in closer to read her words.

For I will always have
For I will always have the smile, the laughter, the memories,

For I will always have the time, the effort, the pleasures,
For I will always have the pain, the tears, ashes in the seas,
For I will always have the love beyond all measures,
For I will always have her and you will always have me,
I know what is taken cannot be given back with leisure,
But I will always have her in my mind for eternity.
For you have shown me this,
For you have taught me to breathe in and out,
For you have shown me how to step back into the world.
For you have shown me all of this and asked for nothing in return,
In return I give you my heart, keep it safe for me.

Thanking you on this day and for all days, all my love, your Isla.

I've never written a poem before myself – not a real one anyway, unless you count the Valentine I was coerced into writing my mum in primary school, thinking the whole 'Roses are red, violets are blue' line was my very own. Apart from that I could hardly claim to be a poet, but I knew when Isla gave me this that it was a special poem, from her heart, totally honest. It was a way of saying what she couldn't at that time, on the second anniversary of Hannah's

177

death. Her own words, in awkward sentences. Somehow poetry lends itself to sad stuff better than normal words.

But now I don't know what to think. Am I mad 'cos she's put my poem up, the one she wrote just for me, so everyone can read it? Am I glad 'cos she's taken down the less-than-flattering photo? Why put up my poem, I don't get it. Does that mean she is sorry, really sorry and realises what she's done? Is she trying to annoy me even more? Is she trying to show the other side of me, to make me seem not just a pisshead bloke, but one with real feelings? Should I feel grateful that she's trying to restore my reputation, whatever it was before all of this?

I am once again on the old familiar territory of being one hundred per cent confused by the acts of the species more commonly known as woman. I wish there was a manual or even a guide book, something to give us poor blokes a hint, a little nudge in the right direction at least. But no, we are left to fumble around in the dark, blindfolded and senseless to their needs, feelings and desires. It's a lottery. I try and pick a winning number as I press call on my mobile. Slightly nervous, it has to be said. Ring, ring, ring, pick up, you know it's me . . .

'Hello?' She sounds unsure; this is unusual.

'Hi, it's me. I'm in the entrance hall. I've just seen the poem . . . why . . . ' Before I can go any further, not that I have a clue what to say next, she interrupts in timely fashion.

'I'm so sorry. Please don't go mental, I put it up to try an' show you how sorry I am 'cos you won't talk to (sniff sniff) me and I (sob! gulp!) love you!'

Well, this is less controlled than I was expecting. This is possibly the most emotional woman I know. I don't really know that many women but if I did I reckon Isla would be the most emotional. She cries so easily and I know it's not put on. Anything can start her off – *EastEnders*, a child on one of the NSPCC adverts, a stray dog, her period (which is fair enough as the whole thing sounds horrendous), and she cries especially if we have an argument.

According to her dad Isla has been crying for weeks now – well, certainly the first week anyway. He told me this in the greatest of confidence as we both knew that if Isla found out he had told me this he could wave goodbye to peace and quiet and an improving relationship with his daughter and face something akin to World War Three. I had been amazed to be hearing such information, in a pub, in broad daylight, with Isla's dad of all people. He had got my number off her mobile when she was in the shower and invited me out for a drink. I nearly fell off the top of the stairs where I was stood when he rang me, I couldn't believe I was having the most surreal conversation with my previous arch-enemy. For most of the conversation in the pub I sat waiting for him to say 'Only joking, now stay away from my daughter, you animal!' Instead it went rather differently.

'We just canny take it any more, Luke. She mopes about the house all weekend, struggles into college in the week, isn't doing her assignments, is no' answering the phone to any of her friends, asks every day, I mean *every day*, if you have called an' you never have, which is understandable, son. I am ashamed of what she did too. We are no' asking you to forgive and forget straight away but could you no' listen to the girl? She's after our sanity.'

He looked the same as he's always done, sounded the same, except what he was saying was new and so was the way he was saying it. He was talking to me like I was a human being, a real live person and not a lump of shit he had trodden in, or a sex-starved teenager who was only after one thing from his daughter, which was a bit too close to the truth for my liking. This was the first conversation we'd had where I wasn't looking around the room for exit signs. I didn't know what to say.

'I don't know what to say. I'm sorry, Mr Kelman, but I don't think I can just go back out with her; this has been really horrible, dump— splitting up with Isla but there was nothing else I could do.'

I knew it wasn't what he wanted to hear and I feared the old wrath of his anger and protective nature towards his daughter so I was shocked when he said, 'O'course, son, we couldna ask you to do that. It's just we're worried about her. Well, I'll leave you in peace. We miss seeing you about the house an' that – well, Liz misses you, anyway. See you later, lad.'

I had expected him to explode and tell me to get my arse around there and make up. I almost felt guilty and considered going home with him there and then. I couldn't stand the thought of her upset, but I wasn't ready to see her yet.

I am abruptly brought back to the present by loud sobs and sniffs. Isla is now sobbing whilst apologising for sobbing. I try and cut in.

'Isla, look, it's OK.'

She can't hear me over the elephant impression she is doing blowing her nose. I try again.

'Isla, are you at home? Stay there, I'm coming over.' Sounding quite masterful I take charge and it stops her crying, which is a bonus, and she sniffs an 'OK'.

ISLA

A week after Luke and I got back together ma mum and I had the strangest conversation. She seemed somehow no' to notice that Luke an' I had worked things out an' that he had forgiven me an' apologised for getting drunk in the first place an' I had apologised for taking advantage of him. All of this seemed to have passed her by. This became clear when she asked me if I wanted to go out with her one evening. At first I thought it was a celebration thing 'cos Luke and I were sorted, then I realised it was a sympathy thing 'cos the suggestion was to go to a counselling session with her. I was close to speechless. No one in our family had ever been to a counsellor before.

'But, Mum, I wasna that depressed, an' Luke an' I are all right now, we've made up, we're going out together again. Don't worry about me.' I felt like I had to spell it out for her, she seemed so slow to catch on to what was going on in ma life. Why would I need counselling now?

'What? I am not talking about Luke. It's group counselling for grief.'

Oh ma God! I was so shocked I didna know what to do. Whether to shout at her for suggesting such a thing, hug her for feeling she needed to go or call ma dad for help.

'Please come, Isla,' she said in a small voice which as much as I wanted to I couldna say no to. She looked like she needed support in this and as I was so fine I thought the least I could do was go with her. She was obviously nervous about going somewhere new, somewhere like this on her own.

How wrong I was. I don't know what ma mum told ma dad but he shouted 'Bye' from the shop quite happily so he couldna have had any idea where we were going. We drove to a community centre five miles away and parked in the carpark. I think I must have been more nervous than ma mum an' it wasna even me who needed to go.

We went in an' got chairs an' sat in a circle with about twenty other people who were all laughing an' talking an' looked, well, normal. They didna look as if they had lost anyone at all. I thought everyone would be crying and wailing. After five minutes of waiting the counsellor walked in. I knew it was the counsellor, 'cos he had a name badge on saying DAVID. Quite informal, then. He started talking about how good it was to see everyone again and welcome to any new people. I looked at ma mum but she wasna looking at me, she was gazing intently at David. I felt uncomfortable.

David started talking about how Daphne had told us her story last week and how well she did. Everyone clapped an' a lady who I presumed was Daphne stood up an' thanked everyone for their support an' announced that she was pregnant an' was due in six months. I wondered what her story had been, who she had lost an' why. It was like watching a soap opera but right in front of your eyes.

Then David announced that tonight a new speaker would be telling her story.

'Liz has been coming to us for a while now but this is her first time speaking so I am sure you will all make her feel safe and welcome.' Everyone burst into a round of applause as I looked around to see who Liz was. I was aware ma mum was shuffling in her seat an' when she stood up I wondered if she couldna cope an' wanted to leave. When she started talking I didna hear her at first but then I started to tune in an' hear her loud an' clear an' I realised that Liz was ma mum.

The new speaker was ma mum. She was not a first-nighter, she had been coming here for ages. I didna have time to be shocked or cross as she was pointing to me, saying ma name. I had to listen.

'This is my eldest daughter Isla, now ma only daughter. My other daughter Hannah died over two years ago in a traffic accident . . . ' David gave her an encouraging nod of the head an' she went on. 'Hannah was nine when it happened. It was a normal Saturday night, Isla was round at her boyfriend's house as we'd had a row with her – as I said, a normal night. Ma husband an' I were doing the washing-up. Hannah was in the lounge writing to one of her pen-pals – she had them from all over the world. Every time we went on holiday she would make friends with someone an' get their address an' add them to her collection, sweet thing.

'She had already asked if she could post her letter that night an' I said no, we'd put it in with the rest of the mail in the morning, we run a post office. But she wanted to do it herself. She must have run out across the road, to the post box on the other side. She wouldna use the post box outside the shop as it was always surrounded with kids, teenagers hanging out an' smoking an', well, she felt embarrassed. She wouldna wait until the morning an' when we were in the kitchen, well, out she went.'

She looked at me at this point as if to ask if she could go on. I had not heard this – we had never talked about it, about how it happened. I felt sick an' ashamed that I had not asked, or brought it up, how ma sister died. I had been unable to ask an' I know ma mum had wanted to tell me, but I had shut her out. I wanted to know now, in a room full of strangers smiling softly at ma mum to encourage her to go on, to get it out.

'Apparently she didna look before crossing the main road back to the house, an' it was dark an' he didna see her until it was too . . . until he was too close. I was told she died instantly an' she felt nothing, but I can't help thinking she must have felt something, she would have felt it an' been scared, so scared on her own in the dark . . . ' She paused, tears streaming down her face, her throat all closed an' snot in her nose, trapped an' blocked up, pools of mascara tracks on her white T-shirt, making a mess. I looked down an' saw I had done the same – I was soaked, ma face was stinging from the salt, ma skin felt tight from ma tears. I hadna realised I was even crying until I found it difficult to breathe.

' . . . When we heard all the noise, the shouting an' eventually the knock on the door, I had no idea. I know people say "I knew", that when something happens to your kids you know, but I didna. I was so shocked when I went out an' she was on a stretcher, in the ambulance. She was gone already. There was nothing to do but be sick, then ride with her, holding her wee hand in mine, trying desperately to warm it, to make it work, to make her wake up. She looked normal, not asleep, not gone, just normal like she does every day. They hardly spoke to me in the ambulance. There wasna anything to say, no work to be done, no lives to be saved as we drove slowly to the hospital. Even though I knew there was no point an' there was nothing to be done I still hoped that when we got there something would happen, someone would sort this out. I didna even shout. I didna wonder where ma husband was, or Isla, or locking the house, or about the man, the driver who had knocked Hannah over. It was like all thoughts had stopped in there. It was just us, one last time.

'Once we got to the hospital there was nothing but noise, flashing lights, people taking her, me, ma hand, pushing, pulling, shouting, asking, whispering. Endless drivel that didna matter any more, stupid forms an' questions an' people all over the place, an' then I can't remember the next part – how I got home, when, where she was. It just went on and on for days, weeks – endless routine, things to be done, people to be told, people coming round, sending cards, ringing up, bothering us, being too kind, not letting us alone.' She stopped again to look at me an' I didna know what to do or say so I held her hand. She talked more about the night an' what happened after an' why she wanted me to hear it.

Then David said stuff I think, I guess he must have as that's his job, but I didna listen or hear it as I was looking at ma mum an' she at me. We just stared as if too much had been said an' now we would just have to look as that was easier than continuing to speak. What amazed me more than anything was that when we stopped staring David was talking to someone else – someone else's story was being told an' they had all moved on, just like that. I wondered if we would ever be able to do that, move on.

LUKE

Re-sit. Sounds like reject. Not quite good enough to make it through the exams the first time, can't quite spell his name properly, isn't up to much, reading is a struggle, retaining anything of worth or import is a complication that his brain can't negotiate. Poor Luke. I can see what they are thinking, my teachers, and what they are saying is probably worse. Even now when I have got time to revise the call of the TV is deafening, and though I completely know this is my last chance I still find the phrase 'can't be arsed' so suitable. I want to pass, I want to go on to A2s now I have seen the alternative, but that still doesn't make me put down the remote control and step away from the TV guide.

Mum and Isla have launched a campaign to get me to pass the re-sits. It's called 'Let's bore Luke to tears with revision and then scare him with unemployment statistics until he caves in and manages to take some facts into his small brain'. I think Isla wants a project to take her mind off all the stuff at home with her parents. Her mum is still going to the counselling but Isla reckons she doesn't need it herself. I think she's right 'cos she's got me to talk to. Her mum only has Mr Kelman and it's too upsetting for her to talk to him all the time. I don't get as upset as I would if I had been related to Hannah – it's easier for me to distance myself and let Isla talk it through without thinking about myself and how it affects me. It must be harder to listen if you are totally involved yourself. Anyway, I am letting her order me around to give her something to do as she is sorted herself on revision and exams, Little Miss Organised.

I just don't get it. I used to be so clever at school – obviously I kept it quiet, but I found the whole thing dead easy, GCSEs a mere walk in the park. Then AS levels turn up and run me over with their difficulty factor. I wonder if anyone else has this problem. No one warns you or tells you that it'll be so bloody difficult. If they did I reckon everyone would get a job and give up before they started.

Matthew still seems to be here and Easter was over last week. University holidays seem to be different to the ones the rest of the world have and stretch from one holiday neatly on to the next. This is what's keeping me going with this intense revision programme I have got going on (I'm up to two hours a day now!), the thought of all those holidays, living on your own away from parents, in your own house, doing what you want with your mates, all on your own terms. My idea of heaven.

I decide tactfully to ask Matt exactly when he might be going back to uni.

'So when are you going back then?' This subtle approach receives no reply until it is repeated, directed right at the mound that lies in bed all day as it has done for three weeks now.

'Ugh?'

It speaks. I try for a longer sentence this time.

'Matt? Are you there, Matt? I don't mean to be rude, mate, but you stink. When did you last have a wash? When are you actually getting up?' I try the tact again to see if it works. This time it does. The monster rears its ugly head.

'Wow! The hair monster certainly visited you in the night, or is that from yesterday's sloth impression?'

No reply.

'Get up, you lazy arse, and give me a driving lesson. I'll buy you a pint.' Bribery and corruption – it's sad when it comes to this with your own brother.

'All right, all right, Luke, gi's a minute and I'll be there.'

The old pester technique, tried and tested over many years. No man can stand the whingeing tone of the younger sibling. Success. Another driving lesson beckons. I need a few more practices at three-point turns, then on to the dual carriageway I think, if I can get Matt drunk enough to agree. My mum has made it clear she would rather climb Everest in high heels than get in a car with me.

I don't think there is much to this driving lark though, it seems easy enough. The most important bit is choosing your music carefully 'cos you don't want to get caught driving through town with a dodgy CD your mum left in the car. Cliff Richard is never going to be cool or retro or make a comeback so being prepared is the best way to avoid eternal humiliation.

Matt is the best passenger. He just sits there, looking out of the window, occasionally making the odd observation such as 'Slow down, you idiot!' or 'Stop! Red means stopppppp!' which I find quite useful when learning. He doesn't grip the car seat or door-handle like Mum but he does go very quiet sometimes, which is particularly unnerving when I see his hand over his mouth and his eyes closed. He isn't much help then.

Once in the car, I try to talk and drive at the same time but then remember that as a male I can't really multi-task and only have the ability to do one thing at a time. I decide to take my chances anyway.

'What are you doing over the summer? Are you staying up there or coming back here?'

Matt quickly looks over at me, then back at the road, grimacing as a biker gets too close to our car.

'Watch out Luke! You nearly had that bloke off! You need to move over a bit, you're practically taking up the whole road. Um, I dunno, I'll probably stay up there, why?' He moves to grab the steering wheel as I turn a corner, such a control freak. I continue the conversation, which is hard when he keeps interrupting.

'Because I am going to Edinburgh with Isla, for the Festival, and I didn't want Mum to be on her own the whole summer.' Good job one of us is thinking about her.

'Well, you don't need to worry about the first two weeks 'cos she and Chappers will be in Rome, so after that I will come down for a bit, in case anything is going on here, you know, with them. Then, I dunno, she'll be all right 'cos . . . sshhhittt! Stop! Amber means stop, not keep going!' So bossy. I reluctantly slow down after I've gone through the light. I thought amber meant slow down if you can, but if not go for it.

'What's happening after they go to Rome? I thought they were just going for two weeks. Are they going somewhere else as well?' I wait for a reply but nothing happens. I look over at Matt and he is fixated with something outside. I ask again but he ignores me and starts talking far too fast and loud about Edinburgh and the Festival.

'Is she? They are not going to get . . . ? Are they, Matt? . . . Oh oooohhhh.'

ISLA

It was ma mum's idea for me to go up to the Festival an' stay with Auntie Ailsa. I think she thought I need-ed a break an' she an' Dad probably want more time on their own now they are OK again. I heard them the other night, laughing through the walls of their bedroom, a sound which used to make me cringe as I didna want to think what they were up to in there, but it's a welcome sound now as I haven't heard it in a long time, them joking together, almost happy, almost getting there, moving on in small little ways.

I didna think about them needing their privacy too, that there are some things they need to sort out by themselves, we are not always three people in every-thing together. It's hard to think of them as a couple, not as just ma mum an' dad whose sole purpose in life is to look after me and sort me out with ma problems. I forget they have their own stuff too. Going through the photos of Luke's mum an' Mr Chapman's party made me think. I saw ma mum an' dad having a cuddle outside on the swing, amid all the talking an' laughing of the guests, an' I realised that they are two separate people to me an' have their own lives an' own stuff going on. The counselling thing really made me realise this – the fact that ma mum had been going for ages before I knew an' had told these people stuff she hadna or couldna tell me. It made me think about her as more than just ma mum.

The party was good. I wasna expecting it to be good but it was. Luke was even better – he was really happy for his mum once he'd got over the shock that he was going to have four parents, sort of. Matt had guessed that they were going to get married, but didn't know for sure until just before they booked their holiday, then announced the party. Sort of an engagement party, but not really, as they are too old for all of that. An' having the honeymoon beforehand makes it seem different, doing it in the opposite order, like they are no' trying to be a young couple making a fuss about it all, they are just doing it quiet- ly, apart from the party, which was good 'cos it made it easier for Luke. He was grand. He likes Chappers, so do I. I wonder if he'll just move in an' they will all live there or if they'll have to buy a new house? Luke reckons he'll move in as he was there a lot anyway. He seems to be cool about it. Matt certainly is, but it's different for him as he is never there anyway. I wonder if Luke will still like Chappers once he moves in with all his weird science gear an' mad experiments an' school exercise books. Poor Luke. Imagine living with two teachers.

They are getting married at the end of August. I am invited as are ma mum an' dad, which I thought was nice as Luke's mum doesna know them that well. I have never been to a wedding before – well, not that I remember. Apparently when I was wee I was a flower girl for ma mum's cousin, an' I had to hold the train but I kept playing with it instead, all up the aisle, making whooshing noises with it, pretending it was a wave of the sea washing over me. Everyone thought I was very cute an' took photos, especially ma mum an' dad, keeping the evidence for when they needed to blackmail me, no doubt. Parents shouldna be allowed, should they?

They are getting married in a wee registry office, in Maidstone. That's what you seem to do on your second marriage – have a quieter affair, no' so in-your-face like first-timers. I canny imagine getting married for a second time, 'cos you think the first time will be it, you don't expect to do it again nearly twenty years later. At least I wouldna if I got married, no' necessarily to Luke, although that would be nice, but I know he now has this thing that all marriages are doomed as 50 per cent of them end in divorce or something scary like that.

I'm nearly ready for Edinburgh, just one exam to get through. I didna need to re-sit a module but I wanted to improve on ma results from January. Luke's done his re-sits an' still finished earlier than me! He thinks they went OK, no' good but no' bad, no' like his first attempt. Thank God they let us have a go at the AS exams in January, so then if you mess them up like Luke you get another go in June. I think he actually did a wee bit of work this time round, although most of it revolved around ringing me up to try an' distract me, telling me he needed a break after an hour of solid revision, poor overworked thing.

He is now officially finished for the summer. Year 12 done an' dusted. We're supposed to come back in for lessons once the exams are over but I canny see that happening. It's a stupid idea, Year 12 is finished, so what is there left to come in for? So Luke an' I have elected to spend the rest of July in his back garden or in his room, depending on the weather, conserving our energy for activities of a passionate nature, taking his mum's advice about the whole 'you only live once thing' an' enjoying ourselves, 'cos I know the summer is going to go so fast, an' then it'll be back to normal an' college. I intend to enjoy ma summer, with Luke, in Edinburgh, on our own. I have plans, an' they don't involve any textbooks.

When Isla moves down with her parents from Scotland to England she instantly feels in an alien land. But then she meets Luke. Despite everything (Isla is a motor-mouth, Luke more measured) slowly their friendship blossoms ... and Isla finds that a boyfriend is not only great company but that he can also help soothe a deeper sorrow ...

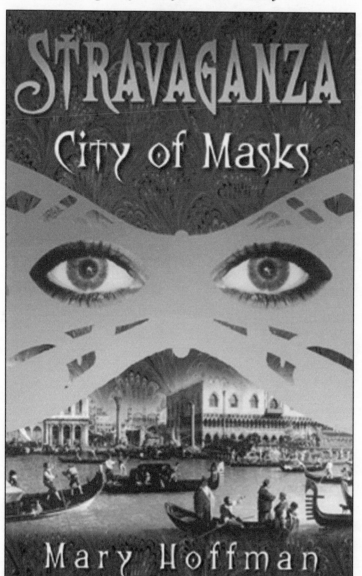

STRAVAGANZA
City of Masks

Mary Hoffman